MW01148133

DEAD IN THE WATER

In *Dead in the Water*, R.J. Patterson accurately captures the action-packed saga of what could be a real-life college football scandal. The sordid details will leave readers flipping through the pages as fast as a hurry-up offense."

- **Mark Schlabach**
ESPN college sports columnist and
co-author of Called to Coach *and*
Heisman: The Man Behind the Trophy

"R.J. Patterson does a fantastic job at keeping you engaged and interested. I look forward to more from this talented author."

- *Aaron Patterson*
bestselling author of SWEET DREAMS

DEAD SHOT

"Small town life in southern Idaho might seem quaint and idyllic to some. But when local newspaper reporter Cal Murphy begins to uncover a series of strange deaths that are linked to a sticky spider web of deception, the lid on the peaceful town is blown wide open. Told with all the energy and bravado of an old pro, first-timer R.J. Patterson hits one out of the park his first time at bat with *Dead Shot*. It's that good."

- Vincent Zandri
bestselling author of THE REMAINS

"You can tell R.J. knows what it's like to live in the newspaper world, but with *Dead Shot*, he's proven that he also can write one heck of a murder mystery."

- Josh Katzowitz
NFL writer for CBSSports.com
& author of Sid Gillman: Father of the Passing Game

"Patterson has a mean streak about a mile wide and puts his two main characters through quite a horrible ride, which makes for good reading."

- Richard D., reader

DEAD LINE

"This book kept me on the edge of my seat the whole time. I didn't really want to put it down. R.J. Patterson has hooked me. I'll be back for more."

- Bob Behler
3-time Idaho broadcaster of the year
and play-by-play voice for Boise State football

"Like a John Grisham novel, from the very start I was pulled right into the story and couldn't put the book down. It was as if I personally knew and cared about what happened to each of the main characters. Every chapter ended with so much excitement and suspense I had to continue to read until I learned how it ended, even though it kept me up until 3:00 A.M.

- Ray F., reader

THE WARREN OMISSIONS

"What can be more fascinating than a super high concept novel that reopens the conspiracy behind the JFK assassination while the threat of a global world war rests in the balance? With his new novel, *The Warren Omissions*, former journalist turned bestselling author R.J. Patterson proves he just might be the next worthy successor to Vince Flynn."

- Vincent Zandri
bestselling author of THE REMAINS

Other titles by R.J. Patterson

DEAD
TO
RIGHTS

A Novel

R.J.
PATTERSON

Dead to Rights
© Copyright 2016 R.J. Patterson

This novel is a work of fiction. Names, characters, places, and incidents either are the product of the author's imagination or are used fictitiously. Any resemblance to actual persons, living or dead, events, or locales is entirely coincidental.

First Print Edition 2016
Second Print Edition 2017

Cover Design by Dan Pitts

Published in the United States of America
Green E-Books
PO Box 140654
Boise Idaho 83713

*For Brian, a great friend and a man
with passion for the Deep South*

CHAPTER 1

May 8, 2004
Okefenokee National Wildlife Refuge

WHEN ISAIAH DRAKE AWOKE, he wasn't sure what felt stranger—the Glock G29 in his right hand or the mangled and severed ring finger he held in his left. The shrill call of the osprey circling overhead had startled him out of his nightlong slumber, causing him to sit up. The unsteady ground beneath Drake confused him, as did the water slapping the sides of the fiberglass johnboat. This wasn't the type of vessel he was used to waking up on with such a pounding headache.

He inspected the two objects in his hand more closely. The gun felt about the same weight and size as the one he'd shot earlier in the day, though he wasn't a weapons expert by any measure. The slender white finger with a chipped but manicured nail also looked familiar, but it was difficult to know where he'd seen it since it was so out of place. Regardless of whom it belonged to, the finger appeared in stark contrast to his dark muscular hand holding it. Studying both objects, he tried to think where they could've possibly come from and who they belonged to, though he was certain one owner was more upset about losing hers than the other.

Drake also heard voices nearby. He couldn't see more than twenty feet in any direction due to the morning fog that had settled thick over the Okefenokee swamp.

"Reckon the jackfish will be bitin' this mornin'?" asked one man.

"Maybe when it warms up a little. Billy told me the warmouths have been jumpin' into people's boats," another man replied.

"Now, that's what I like to hear. To heck with fishin'; I'd rather catch 'em."

"You and me both, brother."

The voices grew louder and louder.

Drake looked at the items in his hands, carefully setting them down so as to not make a sound. But the gun clanked hard on the bottom of the boat, reverberating across the water. He held his breath and didn't move.

"D'you hear that?" one of the men asked.

"Sure did," the other man responded before calling out into the fog. "Hey! Anybody out there? We're comin' your way, and we'd hate to surprise ya by runnin' into ya."

Drake remained still, except for slight head movements as he scanned the boat for a paddle. The only thing at his feet other than a gun and a detached appendage was a smattering of blood.

He looked up just in time to see the outline of a small fishing boat trolling toward him, the front hull poised to pierce the fog. Without any other options besides announcing his presence, Drake laid back down and closed his eyes, praying they'd just scoot on by and leave him alone. Drake needed to figure out what was going on before he engaged with anyone in a conversation, especially two good ole boys fishing the swamp.

"Hold on, Jay. Put that sucker in reverse. My phone is ringin'."

"What's wrong with you?" he asked as the motor whirred and whined in a higher pitch than moments before. "I told you not to bring that thing. In ten years, those phones'll be worse than crack. People are already so addicted to 'em that—"

"Shut up, Jay. I'm a Pickett County Deputy, and Sheriff Sloan requires that we keep our phones with us at all times in case of an emergency. And apparently there's an emergency."

"It better be a dang good'un to interrupt our Saturday mornin' fishin' trip."

"Would you shut up? It's my wife."

"That ain't no emergency. Geez, what's your problem?"

Drake remained frozen in the bottom of the boat, which was rocking slightly more now due to the small wake rippling across the water. Yet to Drake, it felt like a tsunami was headed his way, one filled with waves of accusation and guilt. He needed to avoid detection and get to solid ground before anyone could suspect him of murder. Short of paddling with his hands while hanging both his arms outside of the boat, he didn't have any options. He pondered the tactic for a brief moment before concluding that he'd rather not have an alligator chew his arm off.

Just lay still. They'll go away. Everything is gonna be all right.

Another osprey flew overhead and unleashed a series of shrill calls. Drake took shallow breaths as panic washed over him. His heart beat so hard and fast he was certain it was audible. Yet almost a minute passed without him hearing a word from the men in the other boat.

Are they gone?

Drake hadn't been this scared since the first time he lined up to receive a kickoff on the Pickett County football team as a weak-kneed freshman. His coach told him if he could avoid the first wave of tacklers, he'd run right past everyone one else for a touchdown, which is exactly what happened. He'd been avoiding hits and running past people ever since, all the way to the NFL and the Seattle Seahawks where he earned NFL Rookie of the Year honors and led the league in rushing two out of the past four seasons.

Drake's stomach knotted up as he heard the nearby men's mumbling voices again. All he wanted to do was take his coach's advice again: avoid the first wave and outrun everybody else. It was sound advice, though difficult to execute while floating on a boat in the swamp.

He tried to quell his desire to sit up and peer again into the fog to determine just what type of danger he was in. But he couldn't resist any longer.

When Drake sat up, he looked in the direction of the boat, and his eyes widened. The boat was headed straight for him.

"Look out, Jay!" the deputy shouted.

Jay slammed the boat's trolling motor into reverse, squelching their momentum and avoiding a collision. The men's boat backed away slowly as Drake locked eyes with the deputy.

"Isaiah Drake? Is that you?" the deputy asked.

"Tate Pellman?" Drake asked.

"In the flesh."

"Boy, am I glad to see you," Drake said.

"You gettin' some bites this mornin'? Or just escapin' them paparazzis and the bright city lights?"

"Sometimes you just need to get away from it all."

"I heard that. It's what me and Jay are doin'. You remember my little brother, don'tcha?"

Drake nodded cautiously. "I think so."

"I was five years behind you guys, so I was a little dude when you left town," Jay said.

"You grabbed the tees after kickoff, didn't you?" Drake asked.

Jay nodded. "Sure did."

Tate and Jay's boat drifted closer to Drake's. Their bass boat towered above the water with their chairs perched high. Drake grew concerned that they could see down into his boat. He shifted his feet to cover the gun and finger.

"Well, sorry to interrupt your solitude," Tate said. "I'll let you get back to it. Good luck."

"Good luck to you, too," Drake said. He slowly let out a sigh as Jay jerked the trolling motor in the opposite direction and led them away.

Tate's phone rang again, drawing Jay's scornful ire.

"I swear you must put on a dress when you get home," Jay said.

"I'm gonna feed you to the gators if you don't shut your trap. This is an official phone call."

Their voices faded in the swamp along with their boat.

Drake waited until they were out of sight before he relaxed and lay down again. His mind whirred as he ran through a litany of scenarios as to how he could get back to dry ground.

He decided to sit up and nearly tipped the boat over as he turned to his left and noticed Tate and Jay's boat emerging out of the fog again.

"D-Train," Tate called out, using Drake's nickname from

his Pickett County stardom. "I almost forgot to ask you what the fish are hittin' on this mornin'."

Their boat stopped a few feet short of Drake's. Drake looked down as the short choppy waves rocked his jonboat again.

"D-Train? You all right?" Tate asked.

Drake looked up and took a deep breath. "Yeah. Yeah. I'm good. What did you ask again?"

"I was wonderin' what the fish are bitin' on this mornin'. Got any suggestions? What are you catchin' 'em with?"

Tate leaned forward and peered into Drake's boat.

"I sure hope you don't take this the wrong way, but what's a NFL star doin' in a boat like this? I figured you'd at least have somethin' all tricked out."

Drake shrugged. "Tryin' to be smart with my money. I just finished my fourth season and not a free agent yet. I won't make the big bucks until later the end of next season."

"My goodness, D-Train, you ain't even got a motor."

"Well, I—"

"Or a paddle," Jay chimed in.

"What the—"

Drake put his hands up in the air. "Look, I know this seems strange, but—"

Tate stood up and squinted as he stared at the bottom of Drake's boat. "What's that by your foot, D-Train? You mind movin' your leg so I can see that?"

"What? Oh, this?" Drake held up the gun. "It's just my protection against gators." He chuckled. "You know, in case one decides to climb in the boat with me."

Drake put it down.

"No, that's not what I was talkin' about." Tate pointed at his foot. "I was talkin' about that other little thing right there."

Drake slid his foot over the finger, obscuring Tate's view. "There's nothin' else here."

"Not from where I'm standin'. Now, will you please move your leg so I can see what that is in the bottom of your boat there?"

The shallow breathing returned for Drake. He knew there was no way out of this situation, even if he didn't fully understand what it was.

Drake rolled the finger with the bottom of his shoe, keeping it hidden from Tate's line of sight.

"Dang it, D-Train. Pick your foot up. Hold it in the air so I can see what's on the bottom of the boat."

For a split second, Drake considered grabbing the finger and diving into the water. He glanced to his left and noticed an alligator swimming a few feet away. Drake decided he'd take his chances with his friend.

Drake lifted his foot in the air, revealing the finger.

"What in the hell?" Tate asked.

"I'm just as confused as you are," Drake blurted out. "I woke up in this boat and—"

"D-Train, where's your rod? Where's your motor? Where's your paddle?"

Drake put his foot down hard, the sound of shoe to fiberglass echoing across the water. Out of the corner of his eye, Drake watched the alligator flinch but hold his position.

"Look, Tate, I don't know what to tell you. I just woke up a few minutes ago, and I've got no idea what's goin' on."

Tate motioned for his brother to guide them even closer to the boat where they gently collided. He held his hand out for Drake.

"I'm gonna kindly need you to join me on this boat here," Tate said. He pulled out his gun from his side holster and held it down at the water. "Just leave the gun where it is and come get on board our boat."

"But I didn't do anything," Drake said, refusing to budge.

Tate shook his head. "Explain that finger to me then."

"I- I-I don't know where it came from."

"Well, I do. Your fiancée, Susannah Sloan—she was murdered last night."

Drake stared at Tate, mouth agape.

"What? And you think I did it?" Drake said before breaking into a nervous laugh before tears began streaming down his face.

"They found her body this mornin'." Tate took a deep breath. "She was missin' her ring finger, not to mention that big ring you gave her last summer."

"I swear to you, Tate, I didn't do this," Drake said, choking back more tears.

Tate trained his gun on Drake.

"Get in the boat, D-Train. I ain't playin' games with you."

Drake wiped his eyes and then held his hands up in surrender as he stepped up onto the Pellman brothers' fishing boat. Tate tied his strongest fishing twine around Drake's wrists and read him his rights while Jay tethered the jonboat to their fishing boat.

Drake glared at Tate. "I didn't do this. You gotta believe me. Somebody set me up."

"I'll let a jury of your peers decide your guilt or innocence. But from right here, you look mighty dang guilty."

"I swear on my grandmother's grave, I didn't do this."

Drake wanted to be honest with Tate and tell him everything. Just the night before he found out she'd fallen for some slick Jacksonville lawyer. Their breakup was uncere-monious, if not expected. He'd heard rumors of her dating some mystery man from the big city.

"Save it," Tate snapped. "You ruined my fishin' Saturday with my brother."

Drake sighed and hung his head. A half hour later, he was in the back of a deputy's car and being driven away from the swamp in handcuffs.

Drake hated the water, especially the swamp. But he never imagined when he woke up that morning that it'd be the last time he ever drew a long breath of fresh air as a free man. He never once considered the possibility that he would soon be condemned to die.

CHAPTER 2

Present Day

CAL MURPHY DUG THROUGH the antique chest he'd purchased years ago at an estate sale. His wife, Kelly, had won a best-of-three series of rock-paper-scissors a couple of years ago where the winner got to dictate the location of the old trunk. She chose the attic, ensuring that the box housing Cal's memoirs was out of sight when guests came over for dinner.

Cal dabbed his forehead, mopping the sweat off his brow. The mid-summer temperatures outside in Seattle ranged in the pleasant mid-70s. But the Murphy family attic was something akin to an inferno. As he sifted through all the keepsakes he'd squirreled away, each one resulted in a smile—until he found his stash of football memorabilia.

"There you are," Cal muttered, pulling a football card out of a large stack.

Emblazoned in bold letters at the bottom of the card was a name: Isaiah Drake.

When Drake debuted in the NFL sixteen years ago, he was the next big thing. Fresh off a closely-contested bid for the Heisman Trophy which he lost by just a handful of votes,

Drake was selected fifth overall by the Seattle Seahawks in the draft. Why the four teams ahead of Seattle decided not to draft Drake always befuddled Cal. The former Auburn star was the kind of running back you only see once every generation. Cal never forgot the descriptive words of one columnist who opined that Drake "dances across the field with such finesse and grace that you wish you could freeze time to watch him—but he moves so fast you're never afforded such an indulgence."

Drake's first season with the Seahawks was a continuation of the poetry in motion he exhibited while playing on the collegiate level. Despite being a rookie, Drake played like a seasoned veteran. He darted out of bounds to avoid crushing hits but put his head down and ground out tough yards when the situation called for it. But more often than not, he'd leave 70,000 fans slack-jawed in a stadium several times every game after he broke off a beautiful run or hurdled a defender on his way for a touchdown. And for the first four seasons, Drake only got better.

Cal sighed deeply as he stared at the card and shook his head.

Too bad there wasn't a fifth season—or a sixth or a seventh.

"Honey, when are you coming down?" Kelly called from the ground floor. "Maddie wants to have tea with you before we leave."

"Coming."

Cal slid his Isaiah Drake card into a protective sleeve made out of hard plastic and then scurried down the ladder. He closed up the attic and wasted no time in finding Maddie's room, where she'd set a place for him at her table.

"What are we celebrating today?" he asked, sitting down in front of Maddie's table.

"Tea!" she said before proceeding to pour pretend cups of tea for her father and the two stuffed guests seated on both sides of him.

Cal delicately picked up the plastic tea cup and held his pinky out.

"Is this how you're supposed to drink it?" he asked.

She giggled. "Of course, Daddy. You should know by now. We've done this a bajillion times."

Cal enjoyed the moment with his daughter before the conversation turned somewhat serious.

"You know your mom and I are going away again, right?" he asked.

She nodded. "But Aunt Jillian's coming, isn't she?"

"She sure is. You two are going to have so much fun."

As quickly as Maddie's face broke into a wide grin, it sank. "When will you be back home?"

Cal reached across the table and held her hand. "It won't be that long, just a little over a week. I made a little poster for you to count down the days. It'll be fun, plus you'll have a blast with Aunt Jillian."

Maddie smiled. "You're probably right." She paused. "I may not want you to come home either."

Cal exaggerated a jaw drop then grabbed Maddie and tickled her. "Don't you worry. I'll always come back for you."

After he finished playing with her, Cal's phone rang. It was his editor, Frank Buckman.

"When are you coming down here, Cal?" he asked with a growl. "We've got a few things to discuss before you leave."

"Yeah, we'll stop by before we head to the airport. Kelly's just rounding up all her camera gear and we're waiting on her sister to get here."

"Good. We need to be careful how we handle this story.

Wading into one of the most controversial sports stories of our time isn't something to be taken lightly."

"No, it isn't. To be honest, I'm a little nervous."

"You'll be fine. You're a pro. Just don't lose your focus, and you'll be fine. Plus, you'll have your wife with you, snapping some unbelievable photos. It'll be your favorite assignment you've ever had, trust me."

"But the South Georgia swamp? I've read some crazy stories about that place down there."

"What? Did you find articles about The Marsh Monster?"

Cal remained silent for a moment. "Yeah. So?"

"So, those are all just a great big hoax. There isn't some crazy Neanderthal-looking guy running around down there, hacking people to death."

"I wouldn't be so sure."

"I wouldn't either if I'd read those stupid websites. But just remember, Cal, that when it comes to journalism today, the name of the game is clicks, not accuracy. People will quickly forgive you. They all know how easy it is to accidentally snap a picture of their private parts and have it spread all across social media. Or how someone could hack their account and invite all their friends to purchase a pair of sunglasses. If you say it was a mistake, people will believe you."

"If either of us gets eaten alive by some scaly green monster, you'll know where to look for our bodies."

Buckman chuckled. "If that *actually* happened, I doubt I'll be out looking for your body in the swamp. We'll probably just have some type of memorial service for you, maybe put your body in a crocodile-shaped urn."

"That's not as funny as you think it is."

"Loosen up, Cal. You're headed back to the Deep South."

"I know, which is exactly why I'm not excited about it. Perhaps you don't remember me telling you about the time I went to the bayou to investigate the murder of a superstar recruit."

"Oh, if I've heard that story once, I've heard it a hundred times. Just enjoy yourself and come back with a bang-up story, okay?"

"You can count on that."

"Good because that's what I was worried about most. I know your wife is going to get some great pictures that will make your story appear better than it is."

"How much pleasure do you derive in needling me, Buckman?"

"It's immeasurable."

"You're insufferable, you know that?"

"So I've been told, though I don't let it bother me."

"No, you don't," Cal quipped before hanging up.

Cal sighed as he hung up. Buckman never missed an opportunity to give him a hard time. But this wasn't just a hard time. Cal had serious reservations about heading into muddy southern waters again.

"You all right, honey?" Kelly asked.

Her voice startled Cal and brought him back to reality.

"Who me?"

She smiled. "Who else do you think I'm calling *honey*?"

"Yeah, I'm fine. Just a little skittish about getting back to the south, not to mention getting to interview one of my favorite fallen NFL stars. I'm looking forward to it, though I'm sure it will make me sad."

"Don't you worry. Everything will work out just fine."

Cal returned to packing, but several minutes later, the phone rang. He glanced at the screen but didn't recognize the number. For the first several rings, he avoided answering the phone.

"Aren't you going to get that?" she asked.

He shook his head. "I don't know who it is."

"Aren't you the least bit curious?"

"I am, but not right now. I've got more important things to do."

Cal's phone rang again, this time from the same number.

"No, I don't want your stupid business loan," Cal mumbled as he stared at his phone. "I've got enough problems as it is, like I need a new one to keep me awake at night." But he finally relented. "Hello?"

"Cal Murphy?" asked the woman on the other end in a timid manner.

He stared at the phone number again before putting it back up against his ear. "Yes."

"My name is Marsha Frost, and I work with The Innocence Alliance. We work to get innocent men and women off death row and back into society where they belong."

"I'm sorry, Mrs. Frost, is it?"

"Yes."

"I'm getting ready to go on a trip. I don't have a lot of time right now. Can we talk about this later?"

"I know about your trip, Cal. It's precisely why I am calling. I was wondering if you could do us a favor."

CHAPTER 3

CAL PARKED BENEATH THE SHADE of a towering oak bordering the Georgia Diagnostic and Classification Prison parking lot and stepped out of the vehicle. The muggy air combined with the early July heat led him to loosen his tie almost immediately. He locked the car and waited for Kelly.

"Don't you miss the south?" he said as he took her hand.

She smiled and shrugged. "My hair doesn't, that's for sure. But I can't wait to get a glass of sweet tea somewhere."

"As long as it's paired with pulled pork barbecue, I'm with you."

Striding toward the visitor's entrance, Cal felt Kelly's grip tighten. The barbed-wire fence that encircled the grounds and the ominous armed sentries who paced around in towering guard posts felt every bit as intimidating as designed to do. Cal pulled on the glass door leading into the security screening area, holding it open for Kelly.

"We need to get back here more often," she said, patting him on the chest as she walked by. "You've become genteel on me all of a sudden."

Cal smiled and followed her inside.

After they cleared security, they were met by Isaiah

Drake's lawyer, Robert Sullivan. In Seattle, Sullivan was well known for his high-profile clientele and winning cases that faced seemingly insurmountable odds. Opposing lawyers rarely managed to get a conviction against him. And when they did it, the ruling was often symbolic or a slap on the wrist at best. However, Drake's case was Sullivan's lone blemish, at least among his most famous defendants. Not only was it a failure from the fact that Drake was deemed guilty, but Drake was the first major professional athlete to be sentenced to death in American history. A handful of other stars had committed murder, but none drew such a harsh punishment.

In interviews years after the conviction, Sullivan concluded that Drake would've been better served by a defense attorney from the area, someone the jury didn't look on with suspicion. Hal Golden was the prosecutor in the case and was regarded favorably according to all the news reports at the time. And Sullivan was viewed as the big city lawyer who drew suspicion. Cal, who remembered following the trial as a kid, always thought Sullivan came across as slippery if not slimy when he was on television. Perhaps Sullivan's fake tan or perfect teeth that appeared to glisten when he smiled led not only Cal but the general public to distrust Sullivan. However, Cal felt differently upon meeting Sullivan for the first time.

Sullivan offered his hand while smiling warmly at Cal. In an instant, the suspicion Cal felt toward Drake's lawyer vanished. In less than a minute, Cal was wishing he could befriend Sullivan.

"Thank you, Mr. Murphy," Sullivan said before turning toward Kelly, "and Mrs. Murphy. You both look stunningly refreshed after traveling here from the west coast."

Kelly blushed and smiled. "Thank you, Mr. Sullivan."

"Please, call me Robert."

"And call me Cal."

"Of course, of course. So, tell me why *The Seattle Times* is suddenly interested in interviewing my client. I'd always been under the impression that the Emerald City's favorite football player went from hero to pariah the moment the judge read the verdict and swung his gavel."

"I'm not about to dispute that assessment," Cal said. "As you well know, it's not easy to turn the tide of public perception. But I think there is some growing sentiment among people in the city who are starting to question whether Isaiah Drake actually committed the murder he was convicted of, especially as his appeals dwindle and the date of his execution draws closer."

"We haven't exhausted all our appeals yet," Sullivan countered. "There's still hope."

Cal shrugged. "Maybe, but he doesn't stand much of a chance without some heavy hitters making some noise."

"And you consider *The Times* to be a heavy hitter?"

"They're not the only ones examining the possibility that Isaiah Drake's conviction was a wrongful one."

"Oh, really? I'd like to know who else is on board."

"I happen to know that The Innocence Alliance is considering taking on his case."

"That's news to me."

"It hasn't been made public yet, and they've asked me to help them make a determination about the viability of the case."

"Based off this interview?"

Cal nodded. "Yes, and among other things."

"Well, let's hope that he's far more convincing to you

than I was when I presented my case to the jury."

***

CAL STOOD THE MOMENT the hulking fallen idol entered the room. Drake gripped Cal's hand firmly, forcing the reporter to suppress a grimace. Drake looked Cal in the eye and shook Kelly's hand as well before settling into the chair across the table from them.

Kelly discreetly captured some shots of Drake while he and Cal exchanged pleasantries. The dim fluorescent bulbs overhead flickered occasionally, creating an ominous atmosphere. In his mind, Cal could almost hear other photographers from *The Times* complaining about the poor lighting, but not Kelly. She'd make the best of any situation, especially one involving facial close-ups. It was her specialty, and Cal had little doubt her pictures possessed the potential to overshadow Drake's story. That, however, would depend on what the death row inmate had to say about the case and that fateful night more than twelve years ago.

Cal shifted in his seat and slid his digital voice recorder closer to Drake.

"I want to tell your side of the story," Cal began. "I have to be even handed in this feature, so the more forthcoming you can be, the better light I'll be able to cast you in."

"I understand."

"Good. So, before we get to the night of the alleged murder, can you give me a little bit of background on your relationship with Susannah Sloan?"

Drake closed his eyes and winced, surprising Cal. The almost immediate emotion Drake showed appeared genuine. However, Cal couldn't determine if it was out of regret or pure sorrow.

"Susannah and I had a rocky relationship in high

school," Drake said as he looked down at the table, his voice quivering. "I'm almost certain it had nothing to do with me. I know she was in love with me—and not in that fake high school kind of way. It was real. But we were always breaking up and getting back together, probably because of her father."

"Sheriff Sloan?"

"Yeah, that's the one. I always thought he was a fair man, but he was jealous when it came to Susannah. He didn't want her dating a black guy, that's for certain. But with that said, I don't know if I'd go as far as to consider him a racist. Sounds crazy, I know, but he always treated me with respect. Maybe it was because I went to Auburn."

"Was he an Auburn fan?"

"The biggest, at least in Pickett County. If he wasn't in uniform, you'd rarely catch him in anything but orange and blue. I'd get him going when I mentioned Bo Jackson's name. He'd have a grin on his face for the next twenty minutes as he raved about Bo's other-worldly skills."

"Did he try to steer you toward Auburn?"

Drake eyed Cal cautiously. "Not in any illegal kind of way. I mean, there were other players gettin' paid, but I wasn't one of them. I wanted my education and a shot at the NFL. Anything that could've potentially derailed my dreams was shoved aside, including girls."

"But you and Susannah remained friends?"

"She went to Auburn, too, and watched out for me while I was there. We never really dated while we were at Auburn. She was too focused on getting good grades to get into law school, and I was concentrating on improving myself on the field and in the classroom."

"But things with Sheriff Sloan changed?"

Drake nodded. "After I graduated, I could tell Sheriff Sloan's attitude toward me wasn't the same. It made me question whether the only reason he was ever nice to me was due to the fact that I was always either interested in Auburn or attending there."

"From what I've read, you were quite the legend in Pickett County. It'd make sense that he'd want you to play for his favorite college team."

"Yeah, and maybe that's why I was blinded to how others in my neighborhood viewed him. But I never had anything against him . . . until that night."

"Before we get to that, I want you to tell me what happened with you and Susannah . . . How did you move from friends to engagement?"

"Aside from my mother, Susannah was the one constant in my life. She was always there for me. When I was going through a hard time at Auburn, she kept me going. When I was trying to make the Seahawks during camp, she would call me and give me encouraging quotes. She was my rock. I had to marry her. I couldn't do life without her."

"So, what happened?"

Drake's face fell, and he stared down at the table.

"She chased her dream to go to law school and become a prosecutor. And I chased mine in the NFL."

"But weren't you still engaged?"

"Some of my boys had mentioned that they thought she was seeing somebody else, but I didn't want to believe it. I came back to visit with friends and family and talk with her about it before training camp that year. I didn't want to believe she'd betrayed me like that, but I couldn't ignore it, especially after what happened that night at the club."

"*The* night?"

"Yeah, May 7, 2004—the night my life changed forever."

Cal scratched out a few notes. "Walk me through that day, will you?"

"I got up and hung out with my boy, Jordan Hayward."

"What did you do?"

"Got something to eat. Went fishing. Shot a few rounds at the range. Ate lunch. Nothing exciting."

"Then what?"

"I took a nap and then met some more of my guys at The Pirate's Den for drinks. We were all having a great time, drinking and reliving the glory days at Pickett County. When you win a state championship in this town, you instantly become a legend, part of this community's folklore. Pickett County hadn't won a title in more than twenty years before my freshman year. By the time I graduated, we'd won three."

"That's quite a feat."

Drake nodded. "On paper it was, but we should've won four. Our little school had ten guys from those teams go on to play college football; six of us made it to the NFL."

"But you were the only superstar."

Drake shrugged. "I was in the limelight more than the other guys, but they were all very good. You don't make it into the league by being a slouch. Everyone who gets there is a superstar. And even then, you gotta fight like hell to keep your slot on the roster."

"So, back to May 7th. What happened next?"

"After a few drinks, I had to go to the restroom when some guy bumped into me. I didn't think much about it at the time, but when I reached into my pocket to pull out my phone, I realized the dude had put something in there: It was a picture."

"Like a four-by-six photograph?"

"No, it was a picture printed out on paper that had been folded up several times until it was about half that size. I opened up the picture and couldn't believe my eyes."

"What did you see?"

Drake took a deep breath and waited a moment before continuing. "It was a picture of *her*, of Susannah. And she was in the arms of another man. It wasn't innocent either. There's no other way anyone could've interpreted the picture. She was gazing romantically at him."

"So, what'd you do next?"

"I remember storming out of The Pirate's Den and heading toward my car. I jumped behind the steering wheel and sped toward her house."

"Were you drunk?"

"I'd only had a couple of drinks, so I was very much aware of what was going on. But once I got there, it all became a blur."

"How so?"

"I saw her and then I heard some voices, but I still can't remember whose they were. Parts of that night are still so hazy to me. I remember that I rolled over and looked up at her and she had a frightened look on her face. Then everything went black."

"Everything?"

Drake nodded. "I don't remember anything until the next morning when I woke up with a gun in my hand, lying on my back in a johnboat in the Okefenokee. I know it sounds ridiculous, but that's how I felt, like, *what am I doing here? Whose gun is this? And whose* finger *is this?* I was really freaked out by everything."

"So, before you had a chance to investigate on your own what was going on, you were arrested?"

"Arrested, incarcerated, and now headed for death row. Even all my money couldn't buy the kind of criminal defense I needed to beat a murder rap of the sheriff's daughter. I never had a chance."

"Do you think someone set you up?"

"I believe I was framed. I don't care how drunk I was or doped up by whatever those punks put in my system, there's no way I would've harmed Susannah. She was my world."

"Who would frame you?"

Drake shook his head. "I've been thinking about that for over a decade, and I can't figure out who had it out for me that much."

"Maybe it was someone who had it out for Susannah, instead, and they just saw you as a convenient person to accuse."

"You could be right, but I can't even think of anyone who hated Susannah. Everyone in Pickett County loved her."

"If she was the prosecutor, I doubt everyone did."

"That'd be the only logical explanation when it comes to why anyone would target her. For all I know, they could've been planning on killing her that night no matter what and I just happened to come to the wrong place at the wrong time."

Cal took a deep breath and shifted in his seat. "It could've been a crime of convenience, but I'm guessing it was more a crime of passion based on everything I've read about the case."

"That's possible, but it wasn't *my* passion—at least, I don't remember a thing about it, if it was. I can't help but think . . ."

"Think what?" Cal asked.

"Who got to that kid who supposedly said he saw me kill her."

"What kid?"

"His name was Keith Hurley. He was about twelve years old and was a water boy for the football team when I played. The defense convinced the jury that he'd never forget what I looked like. His testimony is what sunk me. Well, that and waking up in a boat with the murder weapon and Susannah's finger in my hand."

"Sullivan didn't try to discredit this Hurley kid?"

"He did, but it didn't turn out like we hoped. It actually made the kid look more credible."

Cal scratched down a few more notes and looked at his voice recorder. "I hate to be blunt like this, but if you didn't kill Susannah, who do you think did?"

"Oh, I don't know. If I had to guess, I'd say it was Sheriff Sloan. He's the only one who could've covered everything up so neatly."

"He'd kill his own daughter? I've got a daughter, and I couldn't imagine doing something like that, no matter how mad I was at her."

"They had a strained relationship to say the least, but I'd be willing to bet she found out something about what he was doing."

"So, you're saying he's dirty?"

"I'm saying go check it out and find out what you can—and do it fast. I don't have much time left before I exhaust all my appeals."

"I'll do my best," Cal said as he stood up.

Drake grabbed Cal's wrist before he could turn away.

"Be careful, Mr. Murphy. Pickett County has a lot of people with a lot of secrets. If you go poking around down there, you might end up like me—or worse."

CHAPTER 4

A TIN BELL CLANKED against the glass door of *The Searchlight*, Pickett County's weekly newspaper, after Cal and Kelly slipped inside early Tuesday morning. Though tidy and well organized, the cramped reception area was unattended. Cal doubted anyone was permanently assigned to manage the trickling foot traffic a weekly newspaper was likely to receive. When he'd worked at a small paper, such duties were doled out based on seniority.

"Remind you of Statenville?" Kelly asked, referencing the small town paper where they'd first met.

"If I hadn't seen the sign when I walked in, I might have thought I'd been magically transported there."

Before their conversation continued, a young man who looked not a day older than twenty walked toward them.

"May I help you?" he asked.

"I hope so," Cal said, offering his hand to the man. "Cal Murphy, *Seattle Times*."

The man eyed Cal cautiously before glancing over at Kelly and giving her the once over.

"What can I do for you and this pretty little lady here?" he asked, shooting a wink at Kelly.

"Well, my wife and I are wondering if we can speak with your editor," Cal said.

"About what, exactly? He's kinda busy at the moment."

Cal tilted his head to the side, peering around the man. A buxom lady was vacuuming the floor behind him, while the only other person in the office was a man seated comfortably at his desk, nursing a cup of coffee and reading a magazine.

"That guy?" Cal asked, pointing at the man in the back.

The young man didn't turn around.

"If you wanna place an ad, I can take the information for you right now. Otherwise, I'm afraid Mr. Arant doesn't have much time for chit chat."

"He doesn't look busy," Cal said as he watched the cleaning lady stop her vacuum cleaner and begin to wrap up the cord.

The young man stood upright and scowled. "Just because we're not a big city newspaper doesn't mean we don't work hard around here and—"

"I'm sorry," Cal said, holding up his hands in a posture of surrender. "I wasn't trying to imply that you don't work hard. I just thought your editor might want to answer some questions for me about the murder of Susannah Sloan."

"Susannah Sloan?" Mr. Arant asked. He stood up and lumbered toward the front of the office. "Did you say *Susannah Sloan*?"

"I sure did," Cal said.

"Tommy, go finish scanning in those pictures I gave you earlier," Arant said, nudging aside his young employee.

Cal smiled and offered his hand. "Cal Murphy, *The Seattle Times*, and this is my wife, Kelly."

Arant shook Cal's hand and then Kelly's.

"Larry Arant, editor of this here fish wrapper," he said as he glanced around the room. "She's not much, but she's what keeps Pickett County honest, for the most part."

Cal nodded. "I understand. We both worked at a small town weekly before."

"Good. So you know I'm busier than a one-legged man in a butt-kickin' contest, right?"

"We haven't forgotten," Kelly said. "Those were some of our most formative years in journalism."

Arant chuckled. "I'm glad you made it out. You either have to own the paper or have a vindictive wife who divorces you to marry the judge overseeing family court and threatens to eliminate visitation to your two kids in order to stick around one of these places."

"Which one are you?" Cal asked.

"Let's just say I wish I owned the paper and leave it at that."

"Fair enough."

"So, what do you want to know about the Susannah Sloan murder case? It was decided a long time ago in court what happened."

Cal pulled out his notepad containing a few questions he'd jotted down.

"Can we sit down? This might take some time."

"Why not? I've got Tommy doin' all the dirty work today before we put out this week's paper."

Arant motioned for Cal and Kelly to follow him into the interior of the building and gestured for them to sit down around a small round table with four chairs. After he sat down, Arant finger combed his thinning gray hair and loosened his tie.

"So, what's this all about?" he asked.

"I'm working on a feature story about Isaiah Drake, and I'm trying to get a better picture of what happened with the trial."

Arant leaned forward, clasping his hands together and resting them on the table. "I hope you don't think that maggot was innocent, because he was guilty as sin."

Cal glanced at his notes. "How so?"

"Isaiah Drake was always a problem around here. I won't even begin to guess how many times Sheriff Sloan let that kid off the hook—and all because the sheriff wanted Drake to play for Auburn."

"Really?"

Arant nodded imperceptibly. "That's all Sheriff Sloan ever talks about, unless of course there's a robbery in town or Mrs. Rollins' cat gets stuck in a tree for the umpteenth time. It's Auburn football this and Auburn football that."

"And Drake was that good?"

Arant laughed. "Good is an understatement. The kid was one of the best talents ever to come out of Georgia. It's sacrilegious to suggest such things in these parts, but I dare say he was as good as, if not better than, Herschel Walker."

Kelly gasped, drawing a sharp glance from Arant.

"A woman who knows football? I like that," he said.

"You don't want her in your fantasy football league, believe me. I know that from firsthand experience," Cal quipped.

"Hasn't this state been waiting for the next Herschel for decades?" Kelly chimed in.

"They've been waiting for another national title, too, but I doubt it's going to happen. It's why I root for a winner like Alabama."

"Okay," Cal said. "Let's stay focused on Isaiah Drake's case. I'm sure you're busy."

"Well, as I was saying, Sheriff Sloan was always mighty partial to Drake, right up to the day he signed a letter of intent to play at Auburn. After Drake graduated, Sheriff Sloan dropped the act."

"The *act*?" Kelly asked.

"Yeah, Sloan didn't care too much for Drake, mostly because he was secretly dating his daughter."

"Nobody knew about this?" Cal asked.

"A few people did, but it wasn't common knowledge—at least among the Pickett rumor mills. I heard that Sloan almost shot Drake one night when he was sneaking into Susannah's bedroom. Almost blew his ear off with a pistol."

"I was told that a portion of his right ear was bitten off while he was wrestling pig," Cal said.

"That makes a far better story than the truth, doesn't it?" Arant said with a laugh. "We have a way of embellishing our tales down here in the swamp."

"Like The Marsh Monster?" Kelly asked with a laugh.

Arant cut his eyes toward her and glared. "No, the Marsh Monster is real—and I'll go to my grave believin' that."

"Give us your take on the trial. What were the highlights?" Cal asked, redirecting the conversation back toward the point of their visit.

Arant took another sip of his coffee. "This town was a zoo with all the national media descending on Pickett like flies on stink. You couldn't go anywhere without getting a camera shoved in your face and some moron from Chicago or New York or L.A. holding a microphone to your lips while they asked you a question. But I guess I can't blame them since the courtroom wasn't large enough to accommodate more than a hundred people, and the judge wasn't about to let it all be overrun with reporters. They still had to get their stories."

"What was the scene like inside the courtroom?" Cal asked as he scratched out a few more notes.

"It's what you might expect in a case like this. A prosecutor seizing the moment and viewing it as his big opportunity to get noticed. A pompous big city lawyer who was confident he'd get his client off. It was intense, to say the least. Both teams of lawyers were always sniping at one another. It was a game of one-upmanship. And it didn't matter if it was about a point of law or whose lunch had just been delivered to the courtroom during recess. Everyone in town grew sick of the incessant bickering and fighting. We were all just ready for it to be over."

"It seems like they got their wish."

"Yeah, the trial didn't last more than two weeks, and the jury came back with their verdict after deliberating less than an hour."

"How did the prosecution win the case?" Kelly asked.

"I'm convinced I could've argued and won that case. Hell, there are tree stumps in the Okefenokee that could've prosecuted Isaiah Drake and got the same result. Isaiah was engaged to Susannah. Susannah started cattin' around on him with some big shot lawyer from Jacksonville. Isaiah came back to Pickett and had been drinkin' heavily when someone gave him a picture of Susannah and her new beau canoodlin'. Isaiah went over to her house and shot her."

"It was really that simple?" Cal asked.

"Look, Isaiah shot her eight times and cut off her ring finger. The prosecution alleged that he chopped it off because she wouldn't give him back the ring. Now, I don't know about that part, but the murder scene photos were certainly gruesome enough to turn everyone angrily against him. Susannah had always been such a sweet girl, and to see her like that, it was just too much."

"Do you think the racial makeup of the jury had somethin' to do with it?"

Arant rubbed his face with both hands and then glared at Cal.

"Pickett's no different than any other town. The people here ain't perfect, but we all get along for the most part. And people are fair minded. There were five black folks on the jury and seven white folks. And the verdict was obviously unanimous. They all still live around here if you wanna go ask them yourself, but they were all convinced that Isaiah did it. This town wasn't divided in the least bit, especially along racial lines."

"No protests or riots?"

Arant chuckled. "God, I hate social media, and I pity reporters like you who have to work in a big city environment. People in Pickett think *Twitter* is a word meaning *stupid girl*. Celebrity sightings here consist of the few football players who go on to play college ball somewhere or Dan Davis, the best farmer in these here parts who could get a yield of two cotton bushels plantin' in cement. All that to say, the two were united when the verdict was read as well as the sentencing a few days later."

Cal flipped through his notepad and sighed.

"The one thing that's bugged me about what I read is that there was never another suspect, even though most of the evidence was circumstantial."

"Where there's smoke, there's fire. You'd have to be pretty sympathetic to Isaiah to think he didn't do this. Everything was there: motive, the murder weapon, the opportunity. The only oddity to the whole ordeal was how Isaiah was found. He claimed he passed out in a boat, still holding the murder weapon and Susannah's finger. Who does that?"

"That strange behavior is the very reason I can't believe there were never any other suspects."

"Why look for anyone else when the man who's the guiltiest is right there in front of you. While I'm not some big city reporter like you, I've covered my fair share of trials living in this town, and there's one constant: In ninety-nine out of one hundred cases, the most guilty-lookin' person with the biggest motive is your man."

"But what about the other one?"

"There are always exceptions."

Cal nodded. "And that's exactly why I'm here."

"Don't look too hard, Mr. Murphy," Arant said as he stood up. "Flippin' over rocks in this town to dig up somethin' that's probably not there is a good way to get on everyone's bad side. Susannah's death was painful for the people of Pickett, almost as much as it was to watch the greatest football player this area has ever seen get sentenced to death. Scabs are there to help us heal. But if you start pickin' at 'em . . ."

"I might just find the real killer?" Cal asked as he stood up and tersely shook Arant's hand.

"You be careful, Mr. Murphy, and you, too, Mrs. Murphy. We're a friendly little town, but we don't take too kindly to strangers stirrin' up trouble."

Cal scooped up his notebook off the table. "If you find the truth to be troubling, this town has bigger problems than us working on a story about a man who claims to be falsely condemned to death."

Cal and Kelly headed toward the door, both stopping just before they exited.

"Thanks for your time, Mr. Arant, and you have a nice day."

Arant was already walking back to his desk and didn't

turn around, throwing one of his hands in the air for a half-hearted wave.

Once Cal and Kelly were outside, Kelly gripped her husband's arm.

"I've got a feeling that Drake was right about this place."

Cal shook his head. "Well, I certainly didn't expect it to be Disney World."

CHAPTER 5

THE PICKETT COUNTY SHERIFF'S DEPARTMENT located two blocks due east from the newspaper was so quiet when Cal and Kelly stepped inside that Cal wondered if the door was left unlocked by mistake. The air conditioning window unit hummed behind them, and a CB radio unit on top of the receptionist desk crackled with unintelligible chatter between bursts of static. But there wasn't a person in sight.

Cal walked up to the desk and looked around. "Hello? Is anyone here?"

A few seconds later, quickening footfalls grew louder until the door behind the receptionist area swung open. A uniformed deputy hung his head as he entered the room.

"I'm sorry, I'm sorry. Mrs. Rollins' cat got stuck in a tree again, and you know how she can be," the deputy said without looking up.

"Actually, we don't," Cal said.

The deputy looked up, his eyes widening.

"Oh, I'm sorry, I thought—"

"It's okay," Cal said. "We're clearly not from around here, are we? Mrs. Rollins must be quite a character."

"Yeah, a character who doesn't know how to keep her cats inside her house."

Another man entered the room through the door behind the receptionist desk.

"Give her a break, Tillman. She's eighty-two years old and doesn't have anyone to help her," he said before turning to face Cal and Kelly.

"I'm sorry," Tillman said. "I didn't mean anything by it and—"

"Tillman, that's enough. Go on back and finish up the paperwork. I'll help this nice young couple."

Tillman scurried behind the door and pulled it shut behind him.

"Now," said the other officer, "what can I do for you two?"

Cal offered his hand. "Cal Murphy, *Seattle Times*. This is my wife, Kelly. We were wondering if we could speak with Sheriff Sloan."

The man spread his arms wide and grinned.

"You got him, in the flesh," Sloan boomed, his deep voice echoing in the room. "Let me be one of the first people to welcome you to Pickett." He then eyed them carefully. "Unless you've been here before . . . and in that case—"

"This is our first time," Kelly said.

"And as you might well imagine, we're not here as tourists."

Sloan put his hands on his hips and shook his head. "I never assume such things here. You might be here to report a stolen car or wallet. Or you misplaced some camping equipment in the swamp and don't know where to turn." He paused. "Or maybe you saw the Marsh Monster."

"We aren't here for any of those reasons," Cal said dryly.

"Then how can I help you?"

"We want to talk with you about Isaiah Drake."

Immediately, Sloan's affable demeanor turned cold and distant.

"That was a long time ago, and I really don't have much to say about it."

Cal took a deep breath. "I know it's a painful topic to you and—"

Sloan banged both fists on the counter. "You know it's painful? You *know* it's painful? Have you ever had to scoop up your daughter's lifeless and bloody body and put it into a bag? If you haven't, you have no idea how painful that was for me."

"I'm sorry, Sheriff. I didn't mean to—"

"To what? Offend me? I'm not offended by any question about my daughter, but I sure as hell ain't interested in talkin' about it."

"I understand, but it'd be helpful for me if you could," Cal said softly. "There are a lot of people who don't know or don't remember the details around that night. And I'd rather get it straight from the source than rehash articles from over a decade ago. I'm just trying to do my job well, sir. And to my knowledge, your side of the story's never been told."

"Who wants to hear what a grieving, bitter old man has to say about his dead daughter?"

"You'd be surprised. It might even help people who are going through the same thing right now. It's not necessarily about getting people to pity you."

Sloan exhaled and glanced upward for a moment. "Fine. I guess I'll answer a few questions for you."

"Thank you, Sheriff. We really appreciate it," Kelly said.

Sloan motioned for them to follow him behind the reception area and toward his office. The rest of the department was filled with open desks, most of them arranged so neatly that Cal doubted they were ever occupied.

Once they reached Sloan's office, the only one with a door, he slumped into the chair behind his desk and gestured for Cal and Kelly to sit across from him. Stacks of paper cluttered Sloan's desk. On the file cabinet behind him, several stained coffee mugs sat atop another mound of papers, which were also surrounded by wadded up cigarette packs and Snickers wrappers. Directly behind Sloan was a framed panoramic picture of Jordan-Hare Stadium, captured moments before the kickoff of a night game. A well-worn blue Auburn baseball cap sat on the corner of his desk.

"War Eagle," Cal said in an attempt to loosen up the sheriff.

"War *Damn* Eagle," Sloan responded. "Just because you know the saying doesn't mean you know *how* to say it."

"It's not my alma mater, but I know a little bit about life on the plains from when I lived in the south," Cal said.

"You used to write for the Atlanta paper, didn't you?"

Cal nodded.

"I thought I recognized your name." Sloan pulled a cigarette pack out of his desk and tapped the package against the palm of his hand. One of the cigarettes tumbled onto his desk, and he put it on his lips before fumbling through his desk drawers.

"Where's that lighter at?" Sloan mumbled.

Kelly reached onto Sloan's desk and grabbed it.

"Here it is, Sheriff," she said.

He took it from her and smiled. "I'd lose my head if it wasn't attached to my neck." He flicked the lighter, and the cigarette crackled to life. After a long drag, Sloan threw his head back and blew a lungful of smoke into the air.

"Hope you don't mind if I smoke," Sloan said, thumping the cigarette against the ash tray.

Cal shook his head. "By all means."

Sloan grinned. "We don't have all those stiflin' regulations you big city folk have. If a man wants to smoke at his work and no one objects, he can smoke at his work."

"Well, where should we begin as it relates to the night of May 7, 2004?" Cal asked, sliding his digital recorder onto the edge of Sloan's desk.

Sloan eyed the recorder and folded his arms. He leaned back in his chair and looked upward as if pensive about Cal's question.

"I was workin' the overnight shift, and it was relatively uneventful. I think we had a domestic dispute that one of the deputies handled, and that was about it. I went straight from the office to the restaurant."

"So you never left the office that night?" Cal asked.

Sloan shook his head and pointed at his chair.

"I sat right here all night long. Just another boring night in Pickett County."

"But it turned out not to be that way."

Sloan nodded in agreement. "That's an understatement. It was far busier than usual when it came to criminal activity, though nothing we knew about until the next morning."

"What happened the next morning?"

Sloan sighed and looked down. "I went over to check on Susannah and found her dead on the back porch." He took a deep breath and looked over his shoulder, fighting the tears. "I couldn't believe it. My baby girl was gone. It was brutal."

"Did you normally go check on her?"

Sloan bristled. "Is this an interview or an inquisition?"

"I'm sorry, Sheriff. Let me rephrase that: What led you to go over there and check on her?"

Sloan exhaled. "We met every Saturday mornin' at eight o'clock for breakfast at Pat's off Second and Main. The night before, she had called me to confirm we were still on and told me she had some big news. I asked her if she was going to tell me she was pregnant, but she just laughed and said she wasn't that kind of girl. I was somewhat relieved. But when she didn't show up, I called her but didn't get a response. Then I decided to drive to her house and check on her. I thought maybe she'd slept in or had a hangover. I certainly wasn't expectin' what I found."

"Do you still have your logs from that night?" Cal asked. "I'd love to see them to give us some context for what happens in this town."

"Why the hell not? It's all public record anyway. If I didn't, you'd probably have some big city lawyer suin' the county."

Sloan got up and opened the door to his office.

"Tillman!" he called. "Help these folks to the archive room. They want to see the logs from May 7 and 8, 2004."

Cal and Kelly stood up and followed Deputy Tillman into a backroom. The walls were made of cinder block, and the file cabinets looked like they pre-dated 1960.

"We keep paper files of everything for the twenty latest years," Tillman said. "After that, they all go into a file box and are stored at the courthouse. The 2004 files are in that third section, top drawer."

"Thank you for your help," Cal said.

Cal and Kelly worked together to dig through the folders, which were haphazardly filed. Instead of being in a chronological position, they were grouped by months. But the twenty-fifth of a month could just as easily be at the front as the first of the month could be tucked away at the back of the group.

After a few minutes of rifling through the papers, they found the logs for May 7, 2004.

"Will you look at this?" Cal said.

Kelly leaned over and studied the page before she gasped. She proceeded to pull out her camera and take a picture of the document.

"Why would he lie about this?" Cal asked.

Kelly shrugged as she stared down at the paper.

Cal slid the page back into the folder. He jotted down the details surrounding the log: Sheriff Sloan had logged out around 9:30 p.m. He returned at 11:00 p.m. The reason for his departure was listed as *personal*.

"Whoa. Can you believe this? Nine-thirty to eleven— isn't that the window for the time of death for Susannah Sloan?"

Kelly nodded. "So we hear."

"Why would he lie about something like that when he knows we're going to check it out?" Cal asked. "He even invited us to look into the books."

"Pull that sheet out again," Kelly said.

Cal complied, and she studied the sheet for a few seconds and then began to nod.

"What is it?" Cal asked.

"That's not his handwriting," Kelly said. "Look here." She pulled out another sheet in the folder that had his signature. "Totally different."

"So maybe someone signed him out."

Kelly nodded. "And since he was conducting the investigation, no one was ever going to ask him about it."

"But he was still covering his tracks just in case."

They put the files away and returned to the main office.

"Did y'all find everything you needed?" Sloan asked.

"We did," Cal said. "But I've got just one more question before we go."

"Fire away."

"You said you were on the nightshift the night of May 7th, 2004, right?"

Sloan stroked his chin. "That's right."

"And you didn't leave the office until the next morning when you went to go meet with your daughter?"

"That's what I said."

"Okay," Cal said. "I just wanted to make sure."

Cal and Kelly thanked Sloan and left the office.

They were on the street for a moment before Deputy Tillman came hustling out after them.

"Mr. Murphy! Mrs. Murphy!" Tillman called.

Cal and Kelly stopped and turned around.

"What is it, Deputy Tillman?"

"I just want to encourage you to keep diggin' around on this story. I'm not so sure I trust Sheriff Sloan myself. Somethin' isn't right here."

"Thanks for the heads up, Deputy," Cal said. "The reason we're here is to find out what really went on that night."

"Good luck, and let me know if I can ever help you."

***

SLOAN STARTED TO WONDER IF maybe he hadn't covered his tracks as thoroughly as he thought based on the way Cal asked his final question. Trying not to panic, Sloan waited until Tillman wasn't paying attention before slipping into the archive room.

Sloan thumbed through the folders until he found the one dated May 7, 2004, along with the other one from May 8.

He immediately perused the logs, searching for what

might have set off Cal's curious line of questioning. And there it was, almost flickering on the page as if it were a neon sign: Lenny Parker signed Sloan out between 9:30 and 11:00 p.m. the night of the 7th. And he knew exactly what someone could infer from that piece of information.

He decided to create a duplicate log for that night, erasing his missteps, even though he knew he didn't really make any. Parker took up this assignment on his own initiative, even after Sloan had warned the young deputy not to do it. Obviously, Parker ignored him. But it was too late to reprimand Parker, who died a couple of years after the incident when he succumbed to the so-called Marsh Monster.

Sloan knew his logs didn't look good, not then nor in a few minutes after he'd have the whole incident covered up, stricken from the official record. If Drake's case ever returned to court, it'd be a big city reporter against him—and all in front of a jury of their peers.

Sloan liked that idea *and* those odds.

But he had to work quick. He couldn't let Tillman see him or anyone else for that matter.

Sloan knew he'd screwed up, but he didn't count anyone investigating *him*. He'd make it all go away—or maybe he'd be the one who went away.

CHAPTER 6

THE FIRST THING CAL NOTICED when he and Kelly stepped into Curly's Diner—aside from the smell of burgers and the sizzling sound coming from the kitchen grill—was a signed action photo of Isaiah Drake playing for Auburn. Sports memorabilia lined the walls, and several banners touting Pickett County Pirate state titles hung from the ceiling. A trio of elderly men sat at the bar, huddled over their food. Trying to catch a smattering of their conversation, Cal could tell they were talking about college football and debating which school had the best chance to win the national title in the forthcoming season.

Cal and Kelly sat down at the bar, leaving two empty seats between them and the trio. They hadn't been sitting down for more than twenty seconds before a large man wearing an apron and a cap ambled out of the back and behind the bar.

"Good"—the man paused to glance at his watch, held his finger up in the air, and mouthed a countdown—"afternoon. Sorry, I had to wait until the big hand reached the twelve before I could say it and really mean it. What can I start you fine folks off with?"

"We'll need a minute to look over the menu," Cal said.

The man slid a pair in front of them.

"Let me get your drink started while you check it out. What would like?" His voice boomed, undoubtedly loud enough for all the patrons to hear.

Cal and Kelly both ordered sweet tea and continued to study the selections.

"You got it."

When the man returned with their drinks, he fished out a small note pad and a pen. "You decided yet? I'm ready whenever you are."

Kelly ordered the Curly Special, while Cal opted for the pork barbecue sandwich. The man didn't write down a thing before retreating to the kitchen.

When he re-emerged a minute later, he wiped his hands on his apron and proceeded to lean on the counter.

"So what brings you two to Pickett?" Curly asked as his gaze darted back and forth between Cal and Kelly. "You don't write for one of them food magazines, do ya?"

Kelly laughed. "I wish."

Cal cut his eyes over at the picture of Drake on the wall. "We're here because I'm working on a story about your hometown hero."

Curly huffed through his nose. "He ain't a hero to many people around here any more."

Cal furrowed his brow. "Yet you still have his picture up."

"Someone has to remind this town about all the joy Isaiah Drake brought us. And I'll be damned if I'm gonna let popular opinion or a bogus conviction tell me how I'm supposed to feel about him. Besides, he was set up. I just know it."

"What makes you think that?"

"I was at the trial, Mr. . . ."

"Murphy. Cal Murphy with *The Seattle Times*," Cal said, offering his hand.

Curly shook Cal's hand and continued, "Well, Mr. Murphy, it was a sham from start to finish. The prosecutor and everyone else in this town had already decided Drake was guilty. There wasn't the kind of evidence that should ever condemn a man to death, but that didn't stop 'em. He was convicted and sentenced to death for the sole fact that the victim was Sheriff Sloan's daughter. But anybody who knew Drake knew that the prosecution's story about what happened that night was ridiculous. Drake loved Susannah, and there's no doubt in my mind someone set up him to take the fall."

"Any idea who?"

"Drake was popular in Pickett, so it wouldn't be a long list. Perhaps a jealous friend, a rival, someone with an axe to grind."

"Got any names?"

A bell rung, letting Curly know a plate of food was ready. He held up his finger and turned around to grab a pair of plates beneath the heat lamp on the counter. He quickly returned, sliding Cal and Kelly's plates in front of them.

"That's not my style to rat out anyone," Curly said, lowering his voice as he glanced around the diner. "I like my business here."

Another customer sat down at the other end of the bar and signaled for Curly's attention. Without another word, Curly darted toward the customer to take his order.

After Cal and Kelly finished eating, Cal reached for the receipt on the counter. But it didn't budge. Curly anchored the paper to the counter with his first.

"Did you folks like your meal?" Curly asked.

They both nodded.

"It was delicious," Kelly said as she dabbed the corners of her mouth with a napkin.

"Good to hear that," Curly responded while shoving another receipt beneath the original. "You two have a pleasant time here in Pickett, and I hope to see you again here real soon."

Cal slapped a twenty-dollar bill on the counter and nodded.

Curly hustled around the counter and held the door open for them as they left.

However, as Kelly stepped out of the restaurant and onto the sidewalk, she was almost bowled over by a man in a wheelchair.

"Hey!" Kelly yelled.

The man continued on without looking back, throwing up his right hand as some vague acknowledgment that he heard her. But he didn't say a word.

"Never mind him," Curly said as he watched the man roll along on the sidewalk. "That's Devontae Ray, the bitterest man in Pickett, if not the entire state. Can't say that I blame him though. He did get hit while riding a motorcycle with his brother. The accident ended Devontae's dreams of being a professional athlete, but he was far more fortunate than his brother, who lost his life in the ordeal."

"Will he ever walk again?" Kelly asked.

Curly shook his head. "That accident was a long time ago back when he was in high school. He ain't ever gettin' out of that chair. And it's a shame. He and his brother could both fly down the field. It was like their feet didn't even touch the ground."

"Thanks for the great lunch," Cal said, shaking Curly's hand again.

"You're welcome," Curly said. "Just be sure you don't outstay your welcome, especially given the topic you came here to write about. You're sure to stir up some emotions that are still raw with people around here."

"I'll keep that in mind."

Curly let go of the door, returning to the restaurant. Now on the street outside, Cal could still hear Curly's voice booming from inside.

They started to walk along the sidewalk.

"What do you make of that?" Kelly asked.

"More like what do I make of *this*?" Cal said, holding up the receipt Curly had given him.

"What is it?"

"A note Curly slipped me. He slid it underneath my receipt."

Kelly took the note and read it aloud: "Talk to Jordan Hayward. Works at Hank's Pawn Shop. Don't tell him I sent you."

"Interesting."

"Yes," Kelly said. "And he underlined the word *don't* twice just to make sure he was clear."

Cal stopped and glanced back at Curly's Diner.

"Thank you, Curly. I guess we should pay Mr. Hayward a little visit."

CHAPTER 7

HANK'S PAWN SHOP SAT on a corner just off Main and Juniper and was accessible from either street. Cal noted the building's white brick veneer needed a new paint job, but that was far down on the pecking order of necessary maintenance. He held the door open for Kelly before they stepped into the store, which wasn't much cooler than the muggy air outside.

Add air conditioning unit to the list of repairs.

Cal stopped in front of a fan for a moment to cool off. He scanned the store's hodgepodge of items for sale. Nothing of considerable value was on the storeroom floor with most of the high-dollar ticket objects encased in a glass display beneath the counter or on the wall behind the clerk. Diamond rings, gold jewelry, bikes, guitars, televisions—all the usual fare.

An overhead light flickered before going out.

And light bulbs need to go on the list as well.

"Can I help you folks?" called a man from across the room.

Cal looked up to see a man who appeared to be in his mid-fifties, hunched over the counter with a bottle in his hand. Cal and Kelly quickened their pace and walked up to him.

"We were actually hoping to find Jordan Hayward here. Does he still work here?" Cal asked.

The man, who wore a khaki shirt with the name 'Hank' stitched over the left pocket, rolled his eyes and shook his head. "We both wish he didn't, but I can't find anyone else to work in this hell hole, and nobody in town'll hire him."

Cal cocked his head to one side. "So is he here?"

Hank let out an exasperated breath before putting the bottle to his lips and spewing a long stream of tobacco juice into it. A flimsy strand of saliva momentarily hung between the man's chin and his bottle.

"Gimme a second, and let me see if I can find him," Hank mumbled. "He's due for a fifteen-minute break here in a bit. And if he wants to waste it by talkin' with you, that's his choice."

Hank exited the main room by pushing his way through a sheet of heavy opaque plastic strips hanging from the top of the doorway.

"Ole Hank doesn't look too excited to be here, does he?" Kelly asked with a wry grin.

Cal's eyebrows shot upward. "That's an understatement. The fact that this place exists is nothing short of a miracle."

A few seconds later, Hank emerged from the back.

"Just go outside and use the alleyway to your right to reach the back of the store," Hank said, gesturing toward the door. "Jordan is takin' a smoke break but said he'll talk with ya."

Cal and Kelly followed Hank's direction and found Jordan Hayward right where Hank said his employee would be.

Perched on a concrete step, Hayward didn't look up to acknowledge his visitors. A plume of vapor arose around him and swirled away into the light breeze blowing through the alleyway. Holding his electronic vaporizer in one hand, he tugged his hat down with his other.

"Jordan Hayward?" Cal asked.

"Who's asking?" Hayward mumbled, head still down.

"I'm Cal Murphy, and this is my wife, Kelly. We're with *The Seattle Times* and wanted to speak with you for a few moments about something."

"You gotta be more specific than that," Hayward said as he yanked on the tongue of his right sneaker. "I don't just talk with anybody."

"We want to talk with you about Isaiah Drake."

Hayward slowly raised his head, his eyes meeting Cal's with a vacant stare.

"What about him?" Hayward asked with a sneer before releasing another cloud of vaporized nicotine into the air.

"Just trying to find out what happened on the night of Susannah Sloan's murder," Cal said.

"I told the police everything I remembered about that night back when it happened and—"

Cal held up both of his hands. "I don't doubt you did, but I'm retracing all of Drake's movements and trying to get a better idea of what happened."

Hayward shook his head as a slight grin spread across his face.

"There really isn't that much to tell," Hayward said.

Cal sat down next to his interviewee.

Hayward scooted to the side a few inches and put his head back down.

"Anything you say can and will be most helpful as The Innocence Alliance determines if they want to take this case," Cal said.

"Innocence Alliance? That group that helps get innocent people out of prison?"

"That's the one," Kelly said.

"Why do I wanna help them, especially since they got the right man?" Hayward asked.

Cal narrowed his gaze. "So you think Isaiah Drake is guilty?"

Hayward released a large puff of vapor that whipped in front of Cal.

"Can you please not blow that in my face? I don't really want to get high."

Hayward looked back up and grinned. "I can tell you know your stuff, Mr. Murphy."

"Vaping marijuana isn't that novel of an idea. People do it all the time in Seattle. But that's another story for another day."

"I'd rather hear it today—right now," Hayward said.

"I'm sorry, but I'll to have to decline," Cal answered. "We have a big day still ahead of us, and I need to get some answers from some people who were there."

"And what makes you think I was there?"

"I don't know. Just call it a hunch."

"Look, I'll tell you what I told the police and every other reporter and detective trying to figure out what happened that night."

"I'm listening."

"That morning, Drake and I went to get breakfast at Curley's Diner. Heloise had a slow start to her day after throwin' down with her old lady friends the night before and wasn't up."

Cal looked quizzically at Hayward. "Heloise?"

"My mom."

"You were living with her at the time?"

Hayward nodded and continued. "It was just as well, though, because Curly loved Drake and never made him pay for a meal. After that, we drove out to an old abandoned racetrack and saw how fast Drake could go. He'd just bought a sweet new action green Rolls-Royce Phantom. It was hot—but not in the street term sense of the word. He was good with his money, but cars were his weakness."

"So, you raced at the track?"

"Yeah, until Drake hit a pot hole. That ended the racing."

"What happened next?" Cal asked, scribbling down a few notes.

"He dropped me off and said he had some business to attend to and that he'd meet up with me later at The Pirate's Den."

"What time did he get there?"

"He got there somewhere around eight o'clock," Hayward said before taking a long drag on his vaporizer. "I don't know exactly what time because I didn't get there until eight-thirty."

"Did you see him leave?"

"Yeah, he left in a huff. We all saw it. He went to get a drink, but on his way to the bar, he stopped and pulled something out of his pocket. He looked at it and got really mad. Next thing I know, he's storming toward the door like he's jonesing for a fight."

"Did you go after him?"

"Of course I did. I wasn't going to let my boy fight someone on his own. But by the time I got out there, he was gone."

"I drove around looking for him before I decided to

cruise by Susannah's house and see if he was there. His car was parked out front, and I thought about ringing the doorbell. But I didn't want to bother him, so I just went back to The Pirate's Den after that."

"Did you see him again later that night?"

"Nope. Next thing I know, I get a phone call from a friend telling me Susannah was dead and the sheriff arrested Drake."

Cal shot Kelly a look. She nodded, giving Cal the go-ahead to ask the next question they both knew he wanted to ask.

"Drake told me that you went to the shooting range together that day. Do you recall that?"

Hayward shook his head. "I don't remember that. I know we went out and shot a few rounds the day before, but the day of . . . I don't remember that. He probably got his days mixed up. But can you blame him?"

Cal shrugged. "So, are you in the habit of giving out your guns?"

Hayward scowled and took another long drag on his vaporizer.

"It was Drake. What was I supposed to do? Tell him *no*? Nobody tells Drake *no*. He gets whatever he wants, whenever he wants it."

Hayward stood up and nodded toward the back entrance of the pawn shop.

"I gotta get goin'. I hope you find what you're lookin' for. Even though Drake was convicted, some people around here still wonder if he really did it or not. But I know he did it."

Cal nodded. "Thanks for your time."

Once Hayward disappeared, Kelly locked eyes with Cal.

"What do you think?" asked Kelly.

Cal looked skyward and exhaled. "I'm not sure what to think any more. If there's one thing I've learned so far, it's this: Somebody is hiding something . . . and we're going to find out what it is."

Kelly sighed. "Of course we are. Just as long as I don't get kidnapped or you get shot, I'm good with it."

Cal smiled wryly. "I can't make any guarantees, but I'll do my best."

He headed back down the alleyway toward the main road, motioning for Kelly to join him. Waiting for her to catch up, he stared at the building's old red brick.

When Kelly finally reached him, Cal pointed at the outer walls.

"This place has been around a while," he said.

But before he could say another word, his field of vision was suddenly impeded by a large poster board sign attached to a yardstick.

What the . . . ?

"The end is near!" shouted a man who held the sign in front of Cal.

Cal pulled Kelly back as the man encroached in their space.

"That's right. Be afraid. Back away. I know you don't want to hear the truth!" the man said.

Cal gave the man a head fake to the right before slipping past him on the left with Kelly in tow.

"You can't escape the inevitable!" the man shouted.

Cal and Kelly quickened their pace and walked back in front of the pawn shop. Standing out by the door was Hank, who was wiping his hands on a greasy rag. He chuckled at the scene.

"I see you two just met crazy Corey Taylor," Hank said. "Just ignore him. He means no harm; he's just our village idiot."

"He's not exactly the poster child for the Pickett County Chamber of Commerce, is he?" Cal quipped.

Hank chuckled and shook his head. "The Marsh Monster isn't givin' up that spot any time soon. But I'd pay money to see him square off against Crazy Corey. It'd be epic."

Cal glanced at his watch. It was getting late in the afternoon, and they still had work to do.

CHAPTER 8

CAL DURING THEIR RIDE ACROSS TOWN to The Pirate's Den, Cal processed aloud with Kelly what they had learned so far. Cal tried to ascribe motive to Drake—and then to Sheriff Sloan and Jordan Hayward.

"You really think the sheriff could kill his own daughter?" Kelly asked.

Cal stared at the green pasture dotted with grazing cows. "I think you know as well as me that it's wise not to put anything past anyone."

Kelly furrowed her brow. "But his own daughter?"

"Maybe not, but he's hiding something for some reason; that much we know—or at least strongly suspect."

"And Hayward? Why would he do it?"

"Jealousy? Revenge? We're still a long way from figuring out the *why*. I'm more interested in the *who* at this point."

"Those two questions are strangely intertwined."

Cal shook his head. "Don't I know that all too well."

He put on his blinker and turned right into the parking lot for The Pirate's Den. The sign by the road was painted red and black, matching the local high school's color scheme. A caricature of a pirate wielding a sword stood atop the main sign. Below, a lit sign with boxed letters advertised the local cover band for the evening and drink specials.

Cal skidded to a stop in the gravel parking lot next to a truck that towered over his rental vehicle. The back mud flaps depicted Yosemite Sam with guns blazing and the not-so-subtle message of *back off*. Cal noted the gun rack in the back and the dirty baseball cap resting on the dashboard.

They walked past a row of motorcycles and toward the entrance.

"This ought to be fun," Cal said.

Kelly smiled. "I've been waiting for you to take me to a place like this for a long time."

"Best date night ever?"

"That remains to be seen."

Happy hour had just begun in earnest at The Pirate's Den, and everyone inside the establishment was reveling in the moment.

Cal noticed a *seat yourself* sign and took a seat with Kelly against a wall, away from all the locals. They hadn't been there more than a minute before a hefty man who appeared to be in his fifties lumbered up to the table.

"First time at The Pirate's Den?" he asked as he pulled a pencil from behind his ear.

Kelly nodded. "What gave us away?"

He smiled and winked. "My name's Burt, the owner of this here joint. What can I get you two to drink? It's Happy Hour, and all drinks are half priced."

"I'll just have a glass of sweet tea," Kelly said.

"Make that two," Cal added.

"All right then. Sweet tea it is." Burt hustled off and returned moments later with their drinks. "So, have you had a chance to look at our menu?" Burt asked as he placed the glasses on the table.

Cal and Kelly ordered and then asked Burt to return because they had some questions for him.

"Y'all aren't lawyers, are you? My ex-wife has been tryin' to squeeze more child support out of me, and I ain't havin' it," he said.

Cal chuckled. "Far from it. We just have a few questions for you about Isaiah Drake."

"Ah, Isaiah Drake, my favorite Pickett County High player ever," he said, nodding toward a pennant on the wall. "Let me put this order in, and I'll be right back."

"This should be interesting," Kelly said to Cal.

"Guys that run places like these always know everyone's business."

They watched as one of the bikers tipped back a pitcher of beer to the raucous chants of his companions. When he finished, the biker took two steps before toppling to the floor.

Burt returned and grabbed a seat at Cal and Kelly's table.

"Sorry about that," Burt said. "They're my best customers, but they can be intimidatin' to people who haven't been around this kind of drunken revelry."

Cal waved off Burt. "It wasn't that long ago that I was in college. No need to apologize."

Burt clasped his hands together. "Good. So, who are you folks, and what do you want to know about Isaiah Drake?"

Cal offered his hand. "Cal Murphy, and this is my wife, Kelly," he said as the two men shook. "We're here on assignment from *The Seattle Times*. I'm writing a story about Drake. He's close to running out of appeals, and my editor sent me down here to write a story about him and what's happened in those dozen years since he was sentenced to death."

"Life has a funny way of stayin' still in the swamp," Burt

said. "Time goes by, but there's no tide around here to measure it by. We all seem stuck in our lot in life. Hell, if you hadn't told me it'd been twelve years since they convicted Drake, I wouldn't have known it."

"So, same ole, same ole?" Cal asked.

"Pretty much. Avoid the Gators and find a job that can pay your bills. That's how the people around here live their lives." He turned around and gestured toward the patrons behind him, imbibing and laughing. "And find joy where you can. Life's too short to be bitter about it all."

"Not everyone around here thinks like you," Kelly said. "We've met a few who take an opposite perspective."

"I pity those people," Burt said. "But you're right—there are a few who haven't yet learned that life is more than money and prestige. Those people fight for scraps at the table."

Cal took a swig of his sweet tea. "So, let's talk about someone from here who didn't have to fight for scraps when he left town."

Burt broke into a grin. "Ah, Isaiah Drake. He was poetry in motion. I loved watchin' that kid run the football. It was like he was dancin' through a minefield. Nobody could touch him. Still the most amazing athlete I've ever watched in person."

"What do you remember about the night of May 7, 2004?" Kelly asked.

"It was a night I wish I could forget," Burt said. "But I've been asked too many questions about it. It's the one date that's seared in my mind more than the day Betty decided to take our kids and split."

"Were you working here that night?" Cal asked.

Burt nodded.

Cal glanced at his notes. "And did you get any sort of strange vibe from Drake?"

"Not really. He and his buddies looked like they were just here for a good time. Nothin' out of the ordinary as far as I could see."

"What about Susannah Sloan? Was she here that night?" Kelly asked.

"Oh, Susannah," Burt said with a sing-song tone accompanied by a wry grin. "She wasn't here that night. After she was assigned the position of county prosecutor, she almost stopped coming in here altogether. Didn't want to fraternize with the enemy, I guess. But I knew her well from all the times before when she used to visit, especially when she was coming home from law school at the University of Georgia."

Kelly leaned forward on the table. "What can you tell us about her?"

"She was a bright girl, a little on the flirtatious side, the type who always had to have a boyfriend. She was super friendly to everybody, which I think got her in trouble sometimes."

"How so?"

"If she was nice to a guy, he'd start to think she liked him. Then Drake would have to lay down the law—at least that's how it went down when the two of them were dating."

Cal wrote down a few more notes. "So, do you know what happened with her after she stopped coming here?"

"Well, she never really stopped coming here."

Kelly furrowed her brow. "I thought you said—"

Burt held up his hands. "Just during business hours. I used to let her in after we closed the place down and ran off the riffraff. She'd talk to me about all her problems. And if

I let her drink long enough, she'd tell me about her romantic interests."

"*Interests?*" Kelly asked.

"Like I said, she was real flirtatious and always found comfort in the arms of a guy. Of course, it never really lasted long—except for Drake . . . and Tanner."

"Who's this Tanner character?" Cal asked as he jotted down the name.

Burt chuckled. "Tanner Thomas, lawyer extraordinaire from Jacksonville. He specializes in personal injury lawsuits. Just a high-dollar ambulance chaser, if ya ask me. He has billboards all up and down I-95 around Jacksonville. I get so tired of seein' his face when I'm on the Interstate I just wanna punch him in the mouth." Burt stopped and shook his head. "What's even worse is that while I'm drivin' to Jacksonville, I sometimes get the treat of listenin' to him as well with his obnoxious radio ads."

"But Susannah was drawn to him?"

"Like flies to a pig pen. She couldn't stay away. Guess he's good lookin' or somethin'."

"Wealthy?" Cal asked.

"Stinkin' filthy rich," Burt said. "He'd sometimes fly up to Pickett from Jacksonville on his fancy jet. It didn't take long before word got around that when that noisy airplane was landin' at the county airfield, it was none other than Tanner Thomas. I think they tried to be discreet about their relationship or at least convince everyone it was just a professional one. Susannah even went as far as to tell people that his law firm was courting her. But the truth is it was just Tanner himself courting her. I guess after all his overtures, she just couldn't resist. Hell, I just might go on a date with him too if he came to pick me up in a jet."

Cal and Kelly both laughed politely.

"So, she was mulling over her options between Drake and Thomas?" Cal asked.

"For the most part. One of her girlfriends told me that she met a new guy two weeks before she died, another lawyer in Jacksonville, some guy who played backup quarterback at the University of Florida before becoming a tort lawyer. It was probably nothin'. But for what it's worth, I do remember my last conversation with her two nights before she was murdered."

"Did you tell the sheriff's office about it?"

"Nah, I didn't want to dish out any gossip before she was even in the ground."

"Will you tell us about it now?" Kelly asked.

"Oh, I reckon," Burt said. "But gimme a sec to check on that table over there."

Burt hustled across the dining room to another table where four men sat with empty glass mugs.

"What do you make of this?" Kelly asked.

"Love triangle gone wrong? Jealousy? It seems likely that one of her lovers had something to do with it."

"Looks like we've got some more people to check out."

"I've never even heard the name Tanner Thomas during the trial either. And I read just about every newspaper report I could get my hands on."

Burt returned to the table and sat down again.

"Sorry about that. Duty calls. Can't ignore some of my best customers."

Cal nodded. "So you were telling us about your last conversation with Susannah."

"Ah, yes. She got really drunk, and the truth elixir was workin' overtime. That's when she confessed that she was distraught about which man to pick. She slapped a pair of diamond rings down on the bar. I then asked her why it was so hard for her to pick Drake after she'd been datin' him for so many years. That's when she looked up at me and shook her head. I remember her exact words like it was yesterday: Burt, I'm not choosing between Drake and some other man. And that's when I realized what was goin' on. She had two marriage proposals *and* a promising career in law, so it was obvious she wasn't interested in becoming arm candy for Drake just to be relegated to a player's wife for the rest of her life."

"Did she tell you that or is that your own conclusion?" Kelly asked.

"She basically said it, just not in those exact words. I can't remember how she phrased it, but that was the first time I ever even considered that she might not marry Drake. I mean around here, a ring on the finger isn't a done deal, but it might as well be."

"So, do you think Drake knew about all this?" Cal asked.

"I didn't tell him, if that's what you're gettin' at," Burt said. "It's really none of my business even if people tell me their life story. Loose-lipped bartenders don't get good tips in small towns."

"Could anyone else have told him?"

Burt shrugged. "It's possible. Susannah's love life wasn't some state secret, but it wasn't common knowledge either. She did her best to remain discreet about what she was doing. As far as I could tell, she wanted to milk her sugar daddy for as long as possible. He'd just bought her a nice car and a huge ring, not to mention always sending her gifts."

Another customer across the room yelled for Burt.

"Duty calls."

"Well, you've been most helpful," Cal said, shaking Burt's hand. "Thanks for your time."

Burt nodded. "If it wasn't Drake, I hope you figure out who the bastard is who did this. It's been a deep wound in this town for a long time now."

"I'm taking this assignment very seriously; that much you can count on," Cal said.

***

A HALF HOUR LATER, Cal and Kelly got into their car and started heading toward the Okefenokee Inn just outside of town near one of the entrances to the park. The sun slipped away on the horizon as dusk turned to nightfall.

"What do you think?" Cal asked Kelly as he glanced at her.

With wide eyes, she shook her head. "I really don't know. If I had to make a decision based off what we just learned from Burt, I'd say Drake did it. He had a strong motive, means, and opportunity."

"Even with all the other shady activities taking place, like Sheriff Sloan? And the possibility that one of the other men Susannah was dating knew about what was going on?"

"That's where it gets tricky."

Cal gazed at the road ahead. "It's further complicated by the fact that Sheriff Sloan was in charge of the investigation. I think any reasonable law enforcement official would perform due diligence in such an investigation. It's apparent that wasn't the case here."

Kelly nodded. "True, but that doesn't mean he got the wrong guy."

Before Cal could protest, he lurched forward in his seat. *What the—*

Cal glanced in his rearview mirror to see the grill of a large white truck pulling back.

"Cal!" Kelly screamed.

Their car started to veer off the road. Cal resisted the urge to yank the steering wheel back in the opposite direction. Instead, he gradually guided the car off a soft shoulder and back onto the road. Once he regained control, he looked up in time to see the truck roar past him.

Kelly had her camera out and was focusing on the truck.

Cal stomped on the gas, but couldn't make up any ground on the truck that was racing down the road.

"Leave it, Cal. He obviously wasn't trying to kill us, just scare us."

"Did you get his license plate number?" Cal asked.

Kelly stared at the display screen on the back of her camera. "Sure did."

"Good. We need to visit Sheriff Sloan first thing tomorrow morning," Cal said. "He's gonna get an earful from me."

CHAPTER 9

WHEN CAL WOKE UP on Wednesday morning, he stepped onto the small porch from his second story room in the Okefenokee Inn. His view consisted of a forested area that included some marshland. The burgeoning sunlight trickled through the thick canopy, casting a warm glow on the raw nature scene in front of him. A pair of white ibises waded into the swamp, pecking at the water in search of food. The birds' actions mesmerized Cal so much that he didn't notice the bloody carcass of a deer lying at the water's edge or the man cleaning it up.

"Hello there," the man called to Cal.

Taken aback, Cal jumped. "Oh, hello," he said, trying remain composed. "I didn't see you down there."

"But ya saw what Gus did last night, didn't ya?" the man said, gesturing toward the dead deer.

"I guess so," Cal said, leaning forward on the railing to get a closer look. "Who's Gus?"

"Gus is our resident gator, though he isn't always so friendly."

Cal laughed nervously. "That's funny. I don't remember reading about him on the website."

The man chuckled as he shoveled the deer into a thick plastic back.

"There isn't exactly a place to list dangerous exotic animals when you're filling out all your information for those websites. Besides, Gus would never hurt a human."

"Guess I'll have to take your word for it."

The man laughed again. "This is the Okefenokee, Mister. It's a beautiful place, but it's still very wild. Anything can happen out here—and I mean *anything*."

"Except for Gus eating another human being."

"There's always a first time for everything."

Cal's eyes widened as he waved at the man and returned to his room.

"Making some new friends?" Kelly asked as she emerged from the bathroom.

"More like trying to avoid some four-legged ones."

She cocked her head to one side. "Such as?"

"Gus the Gator. Step outside if you want to check out his handiwork from last night. He mauled a deer."

"Right below our window?"

Cal nodded.

***

WHEN CAL AND KELLY stepped into the Pickett County Sheriff's Office, Sheriff Sloan was standing behind the counter and leaning on it while he perused a stack of papers attached to a clipboard. He didn't look up when they entered as he remained fixated on the reports in his hand.

"Morning, Sheriff," Cal said. "I need to report a crime."

Sloan didn't acknowledge him.

"It's best not to bother him until he's downed at least two cups of coffee," the woman at the front desk said.

"I don't think you understand. We need to report a crime."

Still entranced by the papers in front of him, Sloan finally spoke. "Let Betty fill out the paperwork for you. I'm sure it was a terrible crime. Now, if you'll excuse me, I've got a busy day ahead."

Kelly stamped her foot. "We were almost killed last night, Sheriff. The least you can do is hear us out. I'm sure you don't want everyone finding out what a dangerous place Pickett County is."

Sloan finally looked up. "Our crime numbers speak for themselves."

"Is this a game to you, Sheriff?" Cal asked. "Because it isn't to us. Last night, a white pickup truck with the license plate of PFB5661 tried to run us off the road. I swerved onto the shoulder and was fortunate to regain control and avoid an accident."

Sloan laughed softly and shook his head. "Sounds like you met Jacob Boone yesterday."

"So you know who this punk is who almost killed us?" Kelly asked.

Sloan nodded slowly. "Yeah, everybody around here knows who Jacob is. He's a few cows short of a herd, if ya know what I mean."

"You're not gonna do anything about it?" Kelly asked.

"Probably not. He's a pain in the ass, but if your vehicle isn't damaged, there's really no use in it. It'd be more of a hassle than it's worth."

Kelly glared at him. "I can't believe this."

Cal put his arm around her in an attempt to calm her down.

"Is it a common practice in Pickett County to gloss over crimes or just ignore them altogether—or maybe even refuse to question the veracity of one's claims?" Cal asked.

Sloan narrowed his eyes and stared at Cal.

"Just what exactly are you insinuating, Mr. Murphy? That

I'm ignoring criminal activity? Or that I'm guilty of committing it?"

"Both."

"Those are lofty claims. Care to elaborate?"

"You're obviously ignoring the fact that someone in your town almost killed us, someone who must be such a constant nuisance that you know his license plate number by heart and—"

"It's a small town."

Cal kept going, "And when we were going through the logs on the night of May 7, 2004, we found that you actually logged out of the office, even though you told us that you never left. In fact, you were out of the office between nine-thirty and eleven that evening. I'm sure you remember what happened during that time."

"I think it's high time you leave this office, Mr. and Mrs. Murphy—and all of Pickett County, too," Sloan said. "We don't have time for the kind of trouble you're trying to bring to this town."

Cal didn't flinch. "Interesting. You didn't even deny it. I guess the logs are true. I wonder what a judge would think about this information coming to light, especially from the sheriff who supposedly conducted the murder investigation."

"That's enough," Sloan growled as he pointed toward the door. "Out now."

Cal eyed Sloan closely. "Remember, it's always better to give your side of the story than to leave the truth up to conjecture. Or is that what you're hoping will happen? Conjecture doesn't hold up very well in a court of law, does it?"

Sloan kept his arm stiff, pointing toward the door. "I said *now*."

"We'll be seeing you around, Sheriff," Cal said.

CHAPTER 10

CAL AND KELLY HUSTLED down the street toward the Pickett County Courthouse in silence. It wasn't until they'd traveled a block before Kelly spoke.

"I think that went over well," Kelly said.

Cal sighed as he kept walking. "That probably wasn't the best idea to confront him right then, but I couldn't help it."

"Sheriff Sloan's absence during that time certainly doesn't look good. Wonder what he was trying to hide?"

Cal shrugged. "It could've been a number of things, but it was something. He didn't just pop out for a late dinner and lie about it."

They finally reached the courthouse and hustled up the steps. Once inside, they spoke with one of the clerks.

"Hi, my name is Cal Murphy, and I submitted a records request a week ago," Cal said as he pushed his driver's license through the small slit beneath the window.

"Just a minute, Mr. Murphy," the clerk said. "Let me see if I can find this for you."

A few moments later, she returned with a file. She put a clipboard into a drawer.

"I need you to sign this form before I can give these to you," she said.

"No problem."

Cal signed the papers and returned the drawer. The clerk then placed the file in the drawer and pushed it back to him. He grabbed the folder and started to read it as he walked away toward Kelly.

"Sir," the clerk called. "Sir!"

Cal spun around and walked back toward her. "Yes?"

"There are eight more folders. Please don't walk away."

Cal's eyes widened as he stared at the files stacked by the clerk's work station.

"Those are all for the Isaiah Drake trial?" he asked.

She nodded. "That's what the request was for."

"Okay. Load me up."

After Cal collected all the folders, he and Kelly retreated to the archives and began thumbing through the files.

"What are we looking for exactly?" Kelly asked.

"Anything that seems out of the ordinary, but let's write down all the names of everyone we come across. People on the witness stand, people mentioned by the witnesses. We need all the leads we can to create a picture of what was going on back then. The newspaper reports only reveal so much."

Cal flipped open his file folder that had copies of documents for all the legal proceedings, including the prosecution's witnesses. He scanned the list of names, recalling everyone until he landed on the final name: Devontae Ray.

"Skim through these reports and see if you can find the name Devontae Ray," Cal said as he handed half the remaining folders to Kelly.

"Isn't that the guy in the wheelchair?" she asked.

"That's the one. I don't remember hearing his name until we got here, so I don't think he was ever called."

"That's curious."

Cal took a deep breath. "Yeah. Why didn't they call him?"

"Maybe he wasn't necessary. Not everybody on the witness list gets called. He could've been more of a liability at the end of the trial if the prosecution felt like they had it. And they could always call him again if they appealed the ruling."

"Good point. But it still seems odd to me. To peg Drake with a first degree murder charge, they needed to prove his guilt several times over without any doubt."

Kelly nodded. "Like I said, maybe they already proved that during the trial and felt like his testimony wasn't necessary."

"You could be right, but I think this is a question we need to pitch to Hal Golden, Esquire, not to mention a dozen other burning questions I have for him."

"Hal Golden—was that the prosecutor in the case?"

"That's the one."

"And how exactly are we going to do that? He doesn't live around here, does he?"

Cal shook his head and smiled. "How do you feel about a road trip to historic Savannah?"

CHAPTER 11

AFTER A COUPLE MORE HOURS of research, Cal and Kelly drove two hours northeast to Savannah for their scheduled meeting with Hal Golden. During Cal's initial research on Drake's case, he'd contacted Golden to see if he would be open to talking about the trial. Golden, who'd since transitioned from his position as a state prosecutor to a partner with Williams & Anderson law firm, readily agreed to answer a few more questions over dinner.

Five minutes before 6:00 p.m., Cal parked and headed toward the restaurant with Kelly. An iconic fine dining establishment, Elizabeth on 37th embraced the city's historic past, much like the rest of Savannah. Golden recommended they meet at the popular restaurant, which was housed inside an early-1900s mansion that had been restored. He told Cal that it was pricey and would break *The Seattle Times'* meager travel budget, but that he'd love to treat them.

After his initial phone conversation with Golden, Cal tried to resist forming any preconceived ideas about the former prosecutor and fought the urge to tell Kelly about his dinner offer. Cal wanted to determine from their conversation if Golden was serious about justice and believed Drake was guilty—or if it was just an easy victory in a big case that could propel him on to other things. Such determinations couldn't be made by simply looking at a person's resume and timeline of employment or a short conversation over the phone, Cal had long since concluded.

"Swanky," Kelly said as she walked toward the restaurant, taking a moment to run her hand down the smooth Tuscan column flanking both sides of the steps. "This is going to blow our dining allowance for today, isn't it?"

Cal shook his head. "Golden's treating us tonight."

"Already trying to buy us off, is he?"

With his hand on the doorknob, Cal stopped and turned to Kelly. "Keep an open mind, okay?"

She rolled her eyes. "You and your open mind."

"Be nice. Put away your pit bull—at least until we get a few questions answered."

"Don't be worried, honey. I promise not to say anything to rile him up."

A hostess led them to a table in one of the back rooms where Golden was already waiting. He stood up as they approached and offered his hand to both of them.

"Please," Cal said. "No need to get up. Good to meet you, Hal."

"This is Savannah, Mr. Murphy. We always stand up when there's a lady in our presence, especially a beautiful one like your wife here."

Kelly forced a smile. "Such flattery—a common trait among slippery lawyers."

Cal cleared his throat to get Kelly's attention. She quickly sat down as a brief moment of awkward silence fell on the trio.

"So, you wanted to talk about the Isaiah Drake case?" Golden finally asked.

"Yes, I'm working on a story about Drake, chronicling the case as well as his time in prison for my paper in Seattle. He was incredibly popular among Seahawks fans, and with his appeals running out, my editor thought it would make a compelling read to recount what happened to him, from the murder to the trial to the prison time."

"I can only tell you about the trial. I've always been into sailing and never had the time to follow football," Golden said while fidgeting with the band on his Rolex.

"You live in the Deep South and don't follow football?" Kelly asked before dropping into her fake southern accent. "Well, I never."

Golden furrowed his brow. "Not everyone sees the draw in such a barbaric sport. In fact, my ignorance of the sport was why I was chosen to handle Drake's case. Too many football fans might have been sympathetic toward him due to his popularity in the south. I confessed that I'd never heard of him and that's how I ended up drawing the assignment."

"No lawyer from the judicial district office where Susannah Sloan worked wanted to take the case?" Cal asked.

"Oh, several wanted to, but the DA for the state thought it would be best to let a prosecutor from the Savannah district take the case. Too many emotional people as Susannah was supposedly *beloved by all who knew her.* So, that's how the case wound up on my desk."

"As I've been sifting through the case, it seems like there were other possible suspects that went ignored during the investigation. Did you question Sheriff Sloan?"

"Remember, Mr. Murphy, I'm a prosecutor, not an investigator. I take what I've been given, and if it looks like a case we can win, we go with it. This case obviously had plenty of special attention publicly, so I was careful about proceeding."

"So, for instance, if the investigator buried evidence or never brought it up, you'd have no way of considering it when it came to determining whether or not you'd prosecute the suspect?"

Golden nodded. They paused their conversation to place their orders before resuming.

"That's how it always works. You have to trust law enforcement and the information they give you. Sometimes we get surprised with sloppy work, but Sheriff Sloan seemed forthright with me about everything. I had no reason to distrust him."

"What if I told you he hid some evidence, certainly the kind that would raise reasonable doubt?"

"Well, Mr. Murphy, that's something you can print in your article, but it's not anything I'm willing to discuss. As any good prosecutor will tell you, conjecture won't get you a conviction."

Kelly shifted in her chair and asked, "But you're no longer a prosecutor, are you?"

Golden shook his head. "I left that gig behind a long time ago."

"I hear the money is much better," she said.

"That's the understatement of the year," Golden said with a soft laugh. "I have far more time to spend sailing, not to mention I can afford a nicer boat."

"More time at a larger law firm?" Kelly asked.

"I work in tort law, Mrs. Murphy. And while it may be looked down upon by some, everyone needs a lawyer at some point in their lives. I just so happen to enjoy taking on large corporations who are taking advantage of people."

Cal scribbled down a few more notes.

"So, one of the specific questions I had about the trial centered around a potential witness in Devontae Ray. Does that name ring a bell?"

Golden nodded. "Oh, yes. I remember that name very well."

"Was there a reason why he never made it to the witness stand?"

"My team debated for several days about calling him to testify but ultimately decided against it. We found out that the defense had a witness who claimed he was smoking weed with Ray that evening before the time of the murder. Ray's testimony could've been held as suspect if the defense's witness testified."

"And that was that?" Cal asked.

"Ultimately, I thought we had a strong enough case that we didn't need to have him testify . . . and I was right."

"Interesting."

Golden placed his napkin in his lap as the waiter put salad plates in front of each person at the table.

"How much longer are you going to be in Pickett County?" Golden asked.

"Three or four more days, a week maybe. However long it takes to get my story."

"Doesn't seem like there's much to get. It was an easy open and shut case, which is probably why we got such a quick verdict. And believe you me, if I never have to go back to that godforsaken place again, I'll be a happy man. A bunch of backwoods rednecks running scared from *the Marsh Monster*."

"I find Pickett quite a charming little town," Kelly said.

"You may not find it that way the longer you stay there," Golden said. "Just beware down there. You never know who might be watching you."

CHAPTER 12

CAL DESPITE ARRIVING LATE back in Pickett, Cal did-n't want to waste any time jumping back into his investiga-tion Thursday morning. He and Kelly scarfed down a continental breakfast in the hotel lobby before leaving the Okefenokee Inn just before 9:00 a.m. Cal planned on inter-viewing Devontae Ray at his place of work, Stumpy's BBQ.

"Think we should've called before heading out so early to Stumpy's?" Kelly asked.

"If they're serious about their barbecue, I promise you they've been open for a couple of hours now at least."

Several minutes later, Cal rolled to a stop in Stumpy's gravel parking lot. Plumes of smoke swirled skyward. The hickory wood chips mixed with seasoning created an intox-icating aroma for Cal. Though he'd eaten just a few minutes before, he felt his stomach rumble.

"I'm hungry all of a sudden," Cal said as he and Kelly walked toward the entrance.

"You just ate."

"I know. It's my barbecue stomach though. It's craving something."

Kelly rolled her eyes and sighed. "I think you missed your calling in life, Cal."

"You do realize my retirement plan consists of us getting an RV, driving across the country, and writing about barbecue."

"I'll be taking pictures, I assume."

"Absolutely. We'll be a team, an unstoppable one."

"Yeah, because once you get all that extra weight going from the pounds you're going to pack on eating barbecue, you'll just keep rolling forever. Not sure I'm down with this retirement plan of yours."

"We've got time to think of something else . . . that has to do with barbecue, of course," Cal said, winking at Kelly as he held the door open for her.

"Sorry, folks, but we're not open for business yet," bellowed a man from the back.

Cal looked around and didn't see anyone. "Hello? Is anyone here?"

A short portly man hobbled out from the back. He picked up his cane off the counter and leaned on it. "I said we're not open yet."

Cal tried to hide his surprise at the man's short stature. "We're not looking for food, not yet anyway," Cal said. "We were trying to find Devontae Ray. Does he work here?"

The man grunted. "Who's askin'?"

Cal offered his hand. "Cal Murphy, from *The Seattle Times*. And this is my wife, Kelly. We're working on a story about Isaiah Drake and wanted to speak with Devontae, if he's available."

"Well, Mr. Murphy, Isaiah Drake isn't exactly a favorite topic of conversation in Pickett. And if you've been here for longer than five minutes, you've probably already figured that out."

"What about the Marsh Monster? You like talking about

him?" Cal asked, gesturing toward a large framed photo of a shadowy figure in the Okefenokee.

"We'll talk about him all day long," the man said, cracking into a wide grin.

He then offered his hand to Cal.

"Stumpy Jefferson," the man said. "I'm the owner of this barbecue joint here as well as Devontae Ray's boss. Sorry for the hard time. I have to keep up appearances."

"That you're a battle axe?" Kelly asked.

Stumpy chuckled and pointed at Kelly. "I like you already. I would've never bet the first few words out of your mouth would've been *battle axe*."

"Looks can be deceiving," Cal quipped. "She's a feisty one."

Stumpy, who was wearing a pair of overalls and a green Florida A&M baseball cap, gnawed on a toothpick.

"Devontae is on the back porch keepin' an eye on the smoker for me. I'll take you to him."

Cal and Kelly followed Stumpy, who moved methodically toward the back door. He put his shoulder into the door and shoved it open. Immediately, Cal noticed the large black smoker puffing the hunger-inducing aroma into the air. He looked off to the side and saw Devontae Ray hunched over in his wheelchair.

"Got some people here to see you," Stumpy said.

"Never seen 'em before in my life," Ray said.

"Hi, Devontae. My name is Cal Murphy and this is my wife, Kelly. We're with *The Seattle Times*. And I believe we bumped into you earlier this week."

Ray eyed them closely. "Whatcha want with me?"

"We're here because I'm writing a story about Isaiah Drake," Cal said.

"I'm gonna leave you to your business," Stumpy said before hobbling back inside.

Ray put his hands on the wheels of his chair, moving himself forward and backward.

"Isaiah Drake? What makes you think I wanna talk about that murderer?"

Cal shrugged. "I think you know more of the story than anyone else does. Am I right?"

"Maybe."

"Wouldn't you like to tell your story?"

Ray closed his eyes and sighed. "It's not easy to think about those things. A woman died that night, and a hero disgraced himself. People 'round here still hate him and wish the state would've executed him a long time ago."

"Would you be willing to talk, just for a few minutes?"

Ray finally relented. "I guess so."

They went back inside, trading with Stumpy so he could continue minding the smoker.

Ray wheeled himself to the table next to a large grainy picture of the Marsh Monster.

Cal glanced at the picture and decided it might be best to loosen up Ray by talking about some Pickett County folklore.

"You ever see the Marsh Monster?" Cal asked.

Ray smiled. "Maybe once." He cocked his head. "You've only been here a few days and you already know all about Pickett County's second most famous resident behind Isaiah Drake?"

Cal nodded. "It's kinda hard not to. I even heard some story about him murdering two girls in the swamp."

"Now that's some scary stuff, right there," Ray said. "Those two girls' bodies have never been found."

"Did you know the girls?"

"Yeah," he said before letting out a long breath. "They were friends of mine from school."

"So you knew them well?"

"I dated one of them once. I was pretty torn up about it when it happened."

Kelly jumped into the conversation. "Does anyone know what happened?"

"Naw, ain't nobody figured out nothin'. They were just goin' home from school, and that's the last time anybody saw them. The bus dropped them off, and they were just walkin' down a dirt road before they vanished. *Poof.* Gone into thin air."

A screen door slammed shut, and Stumpy shuffled back inside.

"Y'all want some sweet tea?" he asked.

Cal and Kelly nodded enthusiastically.

"Devontae?"

Ray shook his head. "I'm good."

Cal turned his attention back toward Ray. "So, I know that you were on the witness list, but you were never called according to the court reports. Would you mind telling me why the prosecution had you on their list? What did you see?"

Ray took a deep breath. "Here's what happened. That night—"

"May 7, 2004?" Kelly asked.

Ray nodded. "That's the one. I was drivin' around and happened to roll by Susannah Sloan's house."

"You knew where she lived?" Cal asked.

"It's Pickett, man. Everybody knows where everybody lives."

"Okay, go ahead."

Ray rocked back and forth slightly in his chair. "I was drivin' by Susannah's house when I saw Drake jump out of his car."

"You're sure it was his?"

"Ain't nobody in Pickett drivin' a Rolls-Royce Phantom but Drake."

"Okay, so then what?"

"He stormed up the steps and into her house. He was actin' kinda crazy, so I thought I'd stick around and watch and see what happened next. I made the block and parked off to the side of the road, well outta sight. But as soon as I got parked, I saw both of them come out onto the back porch, which I could see from where I was. He had a hoodie on and was shaking a gun at her. She lunged at him and then the gun went off, which seemed to surprise him a little bit by how he was actin'. He glanced around, knelt down next to her body for a bit, and then went back inside the house. I stayed there for a few minutes, watchin'."

"You didn't try to help her?" Kelly asked.

"I ain't no fool. Drake's got a gun. I ain't got nothin'. Think I'm just gonna wheel myself over there and help her out? Nah. That ain't happenin'."

"What did you do next?" Cal asked.

"I was waitin' for Drake to leave. Crazy fool with a gun. Who knows what he was gonna do. Once he left the house, he ran down the street and jumped in another car before he took off."

"Who's car was it?"

"Jordan Hayward's."

"So, Jordan Hayward was there?"

"Yeah. The two of 'em ran out together."

Cal's eyes widened. "So, Jordan Hayward was in the house?"

Ray nodded. "They came runnin' out together."

"But you never saw Hayward go in?"

"Nope. Best I can figure it, Hayward went inside while I was makin' the block."

"Why didn't the prosecution ever call you?"

"They said it's because I was smokin' some weed, but I ain't stupid. Jordan Hayward being there presented some problems for them that they didn't want to explain."

"And the defense? They could've called you as well, but they didn't."

"I was told to keep my mouth shut about Hayward's presence."

Cal's eyes widened. "Even when you testified in court?"

"Especially in court."

"Now are you sure it was Drake who pulled the trigger?"

"Pretty sure. I guess it could've been Hayward—and maybe that's why the state didn't want me on the stand. Maybe they thought I would've created reasonable doubt."

Kelly took a long gulp of her sweet tea.

"What do you think after all these years? Was it Drake?" she asked.

He nodded. "I think so, but Hayward has a lot to gain if Drake dies."

"Oh?" Kelly asked.

Drake nodded confidently. "Yeah, Hayward was the beneficiary for Drake, something I learned while overhearing them talk one night at the Pirate's Den."

CHAPTER 13

CAL WALKED TWO BLOCKS to Memorial Park, just off the Pickett square in downtown. With still plenty of people to interview, he decided to send Kelly on her own assignment while he confronted Jordan Hayward again. She discouraged Cal from doing so, but he insisted and used the assignment for The Innocence Alliance as his excuse to trump her concerns.

"We need to find out if there's enough reasonable doubt to at least get Drake a new trial," he pleaded.

Reluctantly, she had agreed with him and drove off toward her intended destination.

When Cal reached the park around 10:30 a.m., Hayward was engaged in a pickup basketball game with a few friends.

Cal watched intently. Hayward called a timeout, grabbed the basketball, and jogged toward Cal as soon as he saw him.

"This is a far better activity than vaping weed," Cal said.

Hayward waved dismissively at Cal.

"If you think my life is all about my next high, you don't know me at all."

"You're right. I don't know you, but I'm trying to get a better picture of who you are."

Hayward laughed. "How? By talkin' to other people? There are a lot of jealous haters in the world."

"I heard you were inside Susannah Sloan's house the night she was murdered. But that's not what you told me."

"I'm not under oath."

Cal's eyebrows shot upward. "So you were at her house?"

Hayward didn't flinch. "Where's that pretty lady friend of yours?"

"You mean my *wife*?"

"Whatever, man. It's the twenty-first century."

"Well, she is my *wife*, not my *lady friend*."

"Whatever floats your boat. Just tell her it's not a good idea for her to be prowlin' around Pickett on her own, if you know what I mean."

"Why? Are you going to do something to her?"

"I'm just sayin' you better be careful. It's not a good idea for a lady to be cruisin' around unescorted."

Cal narrowed his eyes. "Why? Because you might do to her what you did to Susannah Sloan?"

Hayward's mocking expression turned serious. "What are you tryin' to say, huh?" he said before shoving the basketball at Cal.

Cal caught it and nonchalantly spun it on his index finger. "I guess maybe you weren't shootin' with Drake earlier either, were you?"

"What are you—?"

"Stop with the lies, Jordan," Cal said before squaring up to the nearest basket and hitting his shot. "I'm on to you."

"There's a snitch on every corner, even in Pickett. And they're all trying to get their thirty minutes of fame."

"I believe it's fifteen minutes," Cal said.

"Around here, it's thirty."

"Whatever. All I know is that you're lying to me. This

story you've concocted feels very contrived, so much so that I refuse to believe it."

Hayward put his hands behind his head. "Well, you better start because I ain't lyin'. But just you watch: Somebody will try and kill me before the week is over."

Cal laughed. "If they do, I'll know it's you faking it."

Hayward proceeded to double down on his story. "I never shot with Drake, and I was never at Susannah's house the night she was murdered," he said. "If I was, prove it. Find evidence that I was there and produce it. The truth is I wasn't anywhere near him on that night. That much you can count on."

Cal shook his head. "You know, Hayward, I almost believe you. You're doing a great job of selling this. But something doesn't sit right with me."

"It ain't Stumpy's barbecue, that's for sure."

"No, it's not. But it is your attitude and your evasive responses," Cal said. "In short, I don't believe you. I think you're lying through your teeth . . . I just haven't figured out why yet."

"You're gonna waste a lot of time doing that, Mr. Murphy. I already told you the truth; you just have to believe it now."

"I can smell your BS coming from miles away," Cal said. "And it stinks."

"Oh, really," Hayward said.

Hayward stared at the ball for a moment before passing it hard at Cal's chest. Like the last time, Cal was ready. He caught the ball and smiled at Hayward.

"Don't think you're going to intimidate me," Cal said. "You haven't given me much reason to put any faith in you—and I'm going to keep digging through my investigation until I find the information to put you away if you're guilty."

Hayward started laughing and then formed a gun with his hand, pointing it at Cal and gesturing as if he pulled the trigger.

"Watch yo back, Mr. Murphy . . . if you know what's good for you. Might I suggest a speedy exit out of Pickett?"

CHAPTER 14

WHEN CAL WALKED into Curly's Diner for lunch, Kelly was already waiting for him, seated at a booth in the back of the restaurant. She stared intently at her camera, unaware that her husband had even taken a seat across from her.

"Find anything interesting?" Cal asked.

Startled, Kelly nearly dropped her camera, fumbling it for a second before grasping control again. "Don't do that to me, Cal," she said. "You know I don't like it when you sneak up on me like that."

"You need to add a few more tracks to that one-track mind of yours. You're going to miss quite a bit if you keep your head buried."

"This was just too interesting to ignore," she said.

"What did you find at Susannah's old house?"

"Lots of things. For starters, nobody lives there."

Louise, Burt's lunchtime waitress, took their orders and scurried back to the kitchen.

"Really? I thought she built that house."

Kelly nodded. "She did, but apparently nobody around here wants anything to do with it. There was a maintenance guy there cutting the yard, but the house looked really run down."

"And it wasn't for sale?"

She shook her head. "I checked the records online. The last time it was listed as being sold was when she bought it."

"So, it's just been sitting there collecting dust?"

"Among other things."

"Did you get a peek inside?"

"Oh, yeah, and I've got a few pictures. Check these out." Kelly scrolled through several photos on her camera's display screen for Cal. "As you can see, it's a tight space."

"These will go great with the story, especially when we compare them side-by-side with the original images used during the trial. I really can't believe nobody ever moved into that house again."

Kelly shot him a look. "Would you want to live in a house where a crazy murder occurred? Especially if you lived in a small town? All the neighbors would want to talk about when they came over to visit was *where was she killed,* and *is there still any blood left over.* It'd never stop. Would you want to live with that?"

"Good point."

Cal leaned closer to the screen as Kelly continued to sift through some of the pictures she'd taken. However, she stopped abruptly and looked up when the front door banged shut.

Cal looked at Kelly and then in the direction of her gaze.

"Good afternoon, Jacob," Burt said as he wiped the counter. "I saved you a seat here at the bar."

The man glared at Burt but continued walking toward Cal and Kelly's table.

Louise emerged from the kitchen, carrying a couple of plates. She was headed for Cal and Kelly's table but was halted by the man.

"I'll take those for you," he growled, snatching the tray away from Louise.

"What are you doing?" she said, taken aback by his demeanor.

He ignored her and continued his march toward Cal and Kelly.

Once he reached their table, he dropped the tray, sending some of the fries scattering across the table. "Your order's up . . . and so's your time in Pickett," he said. "It's high time you skedaddle from here and crawl back under whatever rock you came from. Do I make myself clear?"

Cal remained composed, unintimidated by the man's threats. "You must be Jacob Boone," Cal said as he offered his hand. "I've heard so much about you and have been wanting to meet you ever since you ran us off the road."

Boone cocked his head to one side and eyed Cal. "I'm afraid you have me confused with someone else."

Cal shook his head. "As a matter of fact, I'm not. I even had your plates run at the sheriff's office. Not that they needed to run your plates. Apparently, you've got quite the reputation for running people out of town . . . and off the road."

"If I'd run you off the road, you wouldn't be sitting here right now."

"Well, whatever the case may be, we're not interested in your threats or your little mind games. We have a job to do—and we're not leaving until we're finished. Do I make myself clear?"

Boone grabbed Cal's glass of sweet tea and drained it before slamming it back down on the table. Putting his knuckles down on the table, Boone leaned forward and loomed over Cal.

"It's best you leave well enough alone. There won't be another warning," Boone bellowed.

Cal didn't flinch as Boone walked away.

"Louise," Cal called, "I'm gonna need a new glass of sweet tea."

CHAPTER 15

CAL AND KELLY ENTERED the Pickett County Sheriff's Office with a sense of purpose. While Cal liked small town life, he detested the corruption and power trips that often accompanied the people holding the most influential positions. His early assessment of the Susannah Sloan murder investigation was that it was amateurish, refusing to delve into the multiple possibilities. For that reason alone, Cal thought Drake deserved another trial. Drake certainly appeared guilty, but the sheriff's office could have chased down more potential killers to eliminate all doubt. As it stood, the sheriff's ham-fisted approach satisfied the burden of proof for the jury of Drake's peers in Pickett County, and Cal found that difficult to fathom.

"Betty," Cal said, "I need to talk with Sheriff Sloan."

Studying a clipboard in front of her, Betty didn't move. "He's not available, Mr. Murphy," she said. "He's in a meeting until—"

"I'll handle this," Sloan snapped as he entered the reception area, interrupting Betty's rehearsed spiel. He eyed Cal. "What do you two want again?"

"I want to talk with you about this murder investigation, maybe get a few questions answered," Cal said.

"Haven't we already been over this? This case was solved more than a decade ago. We don't need to rehash it when a group of Isaiah Drake's peers heard all the evidence and found him guilty. And I certainly don't care for you to waltz into my town and start slinging around accusations, soiling my daughter's good name. You people are sick."

"Please, Sheriff Sloan," Kelly began. "We're not here to stir up trouble for you. But we do care about a man who could possibly be innocent but will be dead very soon if we don't do something about it. Now, as a man who cares about justice, I think you can understand and relate to that, right?"

Sloan dug into his left shirt pocket and fished out a toothpick before jamming it into his mouth. He exhaled and looked her in the eye.

"I know y'all mean well and are tryin' real hard, but I'm not interested in bein' part of your little witch hunt. We got the right man and he's behind bars, scheduled to be executed soon. And the sooner it happens, the easier it'll be for this community to move on. We're tired of the endless stream of reporters entering our town and tryin' to find answers that have already been rehashed dozens of times. If you think you're the first reporters to visit Pickett and put forth some *new* theories about who murdered Susannah, you're sorely mistaken. We've heard them all countless times, and we're tired of 'em."

Cal put his hands up. "Sheriff, Sheriff. Nobody here is trying to cast you in a poor light. Quite frankly, if it was my daughter, I don't know if I could do what you did and refrain from exacting justice. But I just can't help but wonder if there are other possibilities, possibilities that you didn't consider for whatever reason."

"We did our job, Mr. Murphy. And we did it so well, we

even got a conviction—and it's the kind people around here appreciated."

"All I'm saying is that maybe, intentional or not, you buried the truth . . . and now you're going to bury an innocent man. Have you ever considered that possibility?"

Sloan narrowed his eyes and fixated his gaze on Cal.

"You big city newspaper reporters come down here to our little town and think that solving a murder is as easy as goin' for a jog in the mornin'. As easy as pickin' up one foot and puttin' the other one down. Well, let me tell you one thing, Mr. Murphy, when there's a murder like this, especially a high-profile one, you're tryin' your darndest to solve a crime while everyone else is breathin' fire down your neck. The DA wants updates. The media wants update. Hell, the governor called me for updates. Everybody wants it to go away as quickly as possible so they can get on with their lives. And in this case, I was right there with 'em."

Cal caught a glint of a tear in the Sloan's eye.

Sloan continued. "I wanted it all to go away. My little girl was gone, and there was nothing I wanted more than to be left alone so I could grieve. All your questionin' does is rip scabs off wounds that I thought were healed a long time ago."

"I understand, Sheriff. I'm simply trying to answer all the questions I know my editor will ask as well as our curious readers. This piece has to be as comprehensive as it is conclusive."

Cal exhaled and restrained himself from asking Sloan why he signed out of the office between the coroner's estimated time of death that night that Susannah was murdered. This wasn't the time to press Sloan again on his questionable actions. Cal watched Sloan cast a nervous glance at Betty.

"Look, Sheriff, if you didn't get a conviction on Isaiah Drake, who would you have gone after next? In your mind, who was the next likely suspect?"

Sloan slid the toothpick between his lips forward and took a deep breath. "Ain't no doubt in my mind who I would've gone after next."

Cal refused to wait for Sloan to give him a long and drawn out explanation. "Who would you go after then? Who'd be your next prime suspect?"

Sloan sighed and shook his head. "I would've gone after Jordan Hayward."

CHAPTER 16

ON THEIR WAY to Pickett County High School, Cal and Kelly spent a few minutes reflecting on what they'd learned so far. And Cal figured he was no closer to drawing any conclusions than he was after the day they started interviewing people.

"If we think that Isaiah Drake is innocent, something we need to determine not only for the paper but also for The Innocence Alliance, then we need to have an alternative theory. And right now, I don't know who that might be or how you could even begin to unravel a case like this. Drake just looks so guilty."

Kelly perked up. "The problem in this case is you're thinking like a deductive journalist instead of an inductive one."

Cal shot her a glance. "Deduction is the only way to definitively prove something."

"Exactly," she said, raising her finger. "The key word there is *definitively*. If you're going to raise doubt, you don't have to have lock solid proof. The prosecution didn't, did they?"

"The jury thought the prosecution's proof was beyond the reasonable doubt clause."

"Again, that's what they thought. All you have to do is find a thread to pull on in order to create reasonable doubt in the minds of your readers—and maybe enough that The Innocence Alliance will take on Drake's case."

Cal shook his head. "I'm not sure I can do that, Kelly."

"Why not? An innocent man may die."

"Or a murderer may walk free. So far, all I have are my own hunches that Sloan's team conducted a shoddy investigation. But in the end, their conclusion that Drake was the killer may be right."

"Honey, where there's smoke, there's fire."

"Yeah, but just because smoke is billowing over your head doesn't mean you started it."

Kelly nodded imperceptibly. "You have a point."

Cal wheeled their car onto Pirate Drive at 2:45 p.m. and found a spot in the Pickett County High parking lot. They checked in at the front office and received an escort to the football field where head football coach, Cecil Faris, was getting ready for spring practice.

"Coach Faris," Cal said as they approached, "might I have a minute of your time?"

Faris wore a wide smile blemished only by the lump of tobacco wedged between his bottom lip and gum. He looked down to his right and spewed a stream of amber saliva onto the ground.

"What can I do ya for?" Faris asked, offering his hand.

Cal and Kelly both shook his hand.

"Are you two from Atlanta down here to cover the fastest receiver in next year's recruiting class? Clarence Bailey is the real deal. I saw him run down a rabbit once."

Cal chuckled. "No, you've got us confused with someone else. We're here from *The Seattle Times*, and we're working on a story about Isaiah Drake."

Faris took his baseball cap off and scratched the top of his head before wiping his face with his hand. He repositioned his hat and stared blankly at the bleachers behind Cal and Kelly.

"I'd rather talk about the Bailey kid. Much better story."

"Frankly, I would, too, Coach," Cal said. "But, unfortunately, my assignment revolves around Drake. He's almost out of appeals, and I'm trying to write a story about how this all happened."

Faris sighed and crossed his arm. He barked out a few commands to the straggling line of players filtering onto the field. Seemingly ignoring Cal's request, Faris looked over his shoulder and spoke to his guests.

"Bailey's already in the clubhouse ready to go," Faris said with a wry smile. "Probably because he cut his last period class, but who are we kiddin'? He's gonna play in the NFL one day, and it won't matter how much world history he knows. Nobody's gonna care if he knows Bonaparte from Washington when he's racking up points for everyone's fantasy league teams and winning games for his coach. He's gonna be bigger than Calvin Johnson."

"Johnson was actually smart *and* talented," Cal said. "I wrote a piece on his humanitarian efforts and how he used his engineering skills to craft a toilet using native building materials for less than a hundred bucks."

Faris waved him off. "Either way, all of that is far more interesting than talking about Isaiah Drake's story. Maybe I can send you back with something else your editor will like."

"Nice try," Cal said. "If you don't want to talk about it, I understand. But I thought you might be a great source since you coached Drake . . . and Jordan Hayward."

Faris froze and slowly turned his full attention to Cal. "What does Hayward have to do with any of this?"

"That's what I'm trying to find out," Cal said.

"We think he might be involved in one way or another," Kelly said.

Faris laughed. "Nobody on this team wasted more talent than Hayward. The boy couldn't even write his own name without help until the eighth grade. I can't see him being smart enough to pull off an elaborate plot like that by himself."

"So, you're suggesting if he did it, he may have had help."

Faris shrugged. "Maybe, but don't go putting words in my mouth." He spit another stream of tobacco juice into the grass.

"I think that'd be rather difficult around here," Kelly said. "You don't have the Pickett County accent."

"Why?" Faris asked, breaking into a soft laugh. "You can understand me?"

Kelly nodded. "I've lived in Georgia before and have struggled to hear certain accents, but I eventually get it. Yours, however, doesn't match everyone else's."

"I moved down here from Pennsylvania more than twenty years ago and never left."

Cal gestured toward the can of snuff Faris held in one hand while pinching out some moist tobacco leaves.

"The accent may have escaped you, but the tradition of coaching and chewing didn't."

Faris winked at Cal. "That's a universal practice for football coaches." Faris clapped his hands together. "Now, if you folks don't have any more questions, I've got a practice to run."

"Okay, before we go, I actually do have a few more quick questions for you," Cal said.

"Make it quick."

"Can you tell me about Hayward and Drake's relationship when they were in school? Friends? Enemies? Just teammates?"

"Just two talented kids playing on the same team. I know they hung out together a little bit here and there off the field. But they were both decent back in the day. Neither one of them got into too much trouble."

"So, if Drake didn't do it, who did? Hayward with some help?"

"Now you're asking me to make a call on these two young men and accuse one of them as a murderer. I just won't do it. I don't think either one of them did it."

Cal scribbled down a couple of notes on his pad.

"*Think* or *know*?"

"You never really do know about people. But I will say justice isn't always meted out properly in Pickett."

"What do you mean?" Kelly asked.

Faris turned toward her. "I mean, someone always has to get a pound of flesh. And some of the time, people are so mad that they don't care about who's pound of flesh it is. They just want the pound. And when it's the sheriff's beautiful daughter who was beloved by most everyone around here, two pounds of flesh might even be extracted."

"I'd say it was more than that with Drake getting sentenced to death," Cal said.

"On that point, I'll agree with you. But it may have been another case of good ole Pickett justice. I think there were plenty of other people they could've pinned Susannah's murder on. Why Drake was the target is a question that eludes me to this day."

"Care to venture a guess?"

Faris shook his head. "Too many suspects to sort through. And I certainly wouldn't want any of my players, past or present, to think I'm casting aspersions on them, if you know what I mean. It might be me who ends up floating as gator bait in the Okefenokee."

Cal offered his hand to Faris, and they shook before departing.

"Thank you for your time, Coach Faris," Cal said.

Cal and Kelly hadn't gone more than ten yards before Faris hustled up to them.

"One more question for you," he said.

"What's that?"

"Have you looked into Jacob Boone yet? If I were you, that's a good place to start. He'd be my suspect with or without Hayward."

"Why's that?"

"You're the investigative journalist," Faris said. "You figure it out."

CHAPTER 17

CAL WHEN CAL AND KELLY SWUNG by *The Search-light's* office, they found it nearly deserted except for the chipper cleaning lady. Cal was almost certain she was dancing as she vacuumed the floor. When she spun around and realized she'd been caught, her face flushed red.

"Can I help you?" she asked as she removed her ear buds.

"Yes," Cal said. "We were looking for Larry Arant. Is he available?"

"I'm sorry, but everyone is on assignment at the moment. I was told to tell anyone who came in here to check back in an hour or so."

"We were just hoping to go through the archives for a little research," Kelly said.

The woman shook her head. "You won't find anything like that here. This place isn't big enough. You'll find everything you're looking for at the library."

She didn't wait for another response, jamming her ear buds back into place before resuming her cleaning duties, albeit with far less dancing.

Cal looked at Kelly. "To the library it is."

***

THE PICKETT COUNTY LIBRARY appeared to be one of the newer government buildings around town. It had a clean brick facade along with a bronze statue of Carl Pickett, the man who founded the city in 1803. Cal stopped to read the plaque that explained how Pickett had moved to the area from Cambridge, England, and settled the small farming community. He opened trade with local native Americans and created a supply company for other farmers. However, in 1842, Pickett mysteriously disappeared and was never seen or heard from again.

Cal chuckled and pointed to the last line of the plaque. Kelly didn't find it nearly as amusing as he did.

"I don't get it," she said. "What's so funny?"

"He went *missing*. Maybe it was the Marsh Monster."

"Oh, stop it, Cal. You can be so ridiculous sometimes."

"No, no. Think about it."

Kelly rolled her eyes and nodded toward the door. "Are we going in here or not?"

Cal turned serious. "Depends on if the Marsh Monster is in there or not," he deadpanned.

"You're insufferable."

"Didn't you see the motto on the website? 'You can check a book in, but you can't check out.'"

"Oh, Cal. Come on."

Inside the library, Cal and Kelly were greeted by a rosy-faced woman who appeared to be in her fifties with curly hair that was turning gray. The nameplate labeled Mrs. Louise Kirkwood rested at the edge of the desk in front of her.

"Good afternoon," she said. "Can I help you two?"

"I'm looking for a book on how to keep your husband from telling bad jokes," Kelly cracked.

Mrs. Kirkwood stood up and started to walk around the desk.

"That's not a request we get every day, but we do have some books over in our relationship section that might—"

"I'm sorry. I was just teasing. A little joke between me and my husband."

The woman stopped. "Oh, I see. Sorry. I never like to assume anyone is joking when they enter our library. People don't typically do that in here."

"I know, I know. It wasn't appropriate. I understand."

Mrs. Kirkwood crossed her arms and sighed. "So, what *do* you want?"

"We want to see some copies of *The Searchlight* from spring 2004."

Mrs. Kirkwood's eyes widened as she studied Cal and Kelly more closely. "Follow me."

Mrs. Kirkwood led them to a small room in the back that contained a microfiche machine.

"Whoa, microfiche?" Cal said. "I didn't know this was still a thing."

"It's the most space-saving way to keep our newspapers," Mrs. Kirkwood said. "This room may not look very big, but it could contain several centuries of *The Searchlight* in that filing cabinet alone if everything was placed on microfiche. Maybe one day, Mr. Arant will pony up for an archive for *The Searchlight's* website. Until then, this is your best bet."

Cal and Kelly settled into seats next to Mrs. Kirkwood as she demonstrated how the machine worked. Then she removed files from the time of the murder and placed one of the microfiche sheets on the magnifier.

"So, what exactly are you doing here in Pickett?" she asked.

"Is it that obvious that we're not from around here?" Kelly asked, resisting the urge to put on her fake southern accent."

"Very," Mrs. Kirkwood said. "But I can't quite place where you are from? Canada, maybe."

"Close," Cal said. "We're from Seattle, and we're working on a story about Isaiah Drake."

Mrs. Kirkwood nodded knowingly but remained tight-lipped. She stood up and yielded her seat to Kelly, who eagerly began to scroll through the paper.

"What should I be looking for?" Kelly asked.

"Anything about Jacob Boone," Cal said.

"Jacob Boone?" asked Mrs. Kirkwood, who appeared taken aback by the name.

"Yes," Cal said. "Is there something we should know about him?"

"What did you say you were doing here again?" Mrs. Kirkwood asked.

Cal peered hard at the tiny lettering on the screen. "We're working on a story for *The Seattle Times* about Isaiah Drake."

"Then why in the world would you be looking into Jacob Boone? What could he possibly have to do with it?"

"Just following a hunch," Cal said.

Before Mrs. Kirkwood could protest any more, Cal almost jumped out of his seat with excitement.

"Ah-ha! There you are. Exactly what we were looking for. Read this, Kelly."

Kelly cleared her throat and read a photo cutline:

Jacob Boone collects trash along U.S. Highway 1 on Monday. Boone, who only spent three months in prison out of a seven-year sentence, was released early last week on the condition of giving twenty hours per week for the next two years for community service. He will remain on probation for the duration of his original sentence.

"I've never seen a paper use a photo to report this kind of information," Cal said.

"Welcome to Pickett," Mrs. Kirkwood said. "Around here, we don't always do things like everybody else."

"So, what does this have to do with anything?" Kelly asked.

Cal turned to the librarian. "Mrs. Kirkwood, who prosecuted most of the crimes around here during that time?"

"Susannah Sloan, of course. She handled everything. Didn't matter what it was. It wasn't like she was that busy. Pickett isn't exactly a hotbed of criminal activity. Honestly, that's why Susannah's death was so shocking."

Cal turned to Kelly. "Susannah tries to put Jacob Boone away for seven years and fails. Maybe Boone goes after her for revenge."

Mrs. Kirkwood started to snicker.

"I'm sorry. Did I say something funny?" Cal asked.

Mrs. Kirkwood shook her head. "It sounded like you were trying to pin Susannah's murder on Jacob Boone."

Cal dug in his pocket for a quarter to make a copy of the paper. "Well, maybe not pin it on Boone, but at least come up with an alternative theory as to who actually killed Susannah."

"I'm sorry, Mr. Murphy, but you'll be spinning your wheels if you think you're going to find someone else who killed that poor girl."

"Why's that?" Kelly asked.

"Because we all know Isaiah did it."

"What else did *everyone* know?" Cal asked.

"Well, maybe not *everyone* knew this, but it was common knowledge that Susannah and Jordan Hayward were engaged in some"—Mrs. Kirkwood paused to deliberately clear her throat—"extracurricular activities, if you will."

Cal stared at her wide-eyed. "While she was still engaged to Drake?"

Mrs. Kirkwood nodded emphatically. "Supposedly, Susannah broke it off about a week before Isaiah came back to town, but the rumor was Jordan was torn up about it all."

"So, why wouldn't people think Jordan did it?"

"Jordan might be a pot head, but he's no killer."

Kelly turned off the microfiche machine and handed the sheet to Mrs. Kirkwood. "I don't know, Mrs. Kirkwood. Passion will make you do crazy things—even kill someone over it."

"But to kill the woman you love?" Mrs. Kirkwood questioned. "People who knew the whole backstory could never believe Jordan would do such a thing."

"If this is such common knowledge, I can't believe it wasn't raised during the trial," Cal said.

Mrs. Kirkwood cocked her head to one side. "Well, I don't know if I'd say it's *common knowledge*. I do work in the library, and I hear things."

"I thought people were supposed to be quiet in the library," Kelly said.

"These new generation kids don't quite understand such etiquette. I gave up a long time ago trying to make everyone be quiet." She broke into a wry grin. "I hear so much these days, maybe I can turn this into a lucrative blackmail business."

Cal stared at her, unsure of what to say.

"I'm teasing, you two," she said, breaking into a hearty laugh. "I know I said the library isn't a place where people joke around, but you should've seen the look on your faces."

Cal redirected the conversation back toward his burning question. "So, nobody in Pickett really raised the possibility that maybe Jordan Hayward killed Susannah?"

Mrs. Kirkwood shrugged. "You might find a couple, but most people in this town believe justice was served. And it won't be fully served until Isaiah Drake receives his punishment in full."

CHAPTER 18

CAL AND KELLY DECIDED to squeeze in a quick records review at the Pickett County courthouse before they wrapped up their investigation for the day. Kelly remembered something about a marriage license in the court transcripts that she wanted to look at again. Cal agreed that it couldn't hurt to peruse the files one more time.

On their way to the courthouse, Marsha Frost from The Innocence Alliance called Cal to check in on their progress.

"What have you been able to find out so far?" Frost asked.

"I think you might be able to make the case that Isaiah Drake had terrible representation if anything," Cal said. "There's enough reasonable doubt here that I can't believe any jury of his peers would convict him of this crime, much less receive the death sentence."

"What kind of evidence could you give me?"

"Nothing concrete yet, but if you were able to get a retrial, I'm sure you could win it. Heck, I think I could win it, and I'm no lawyer."

Cal waited for Frost's response, one he expected to excite her. Instead, she sighed.

"I don't know, Cal. Getting a new trial isn't easy. Judges

don't tend to just order retrials without good cause. The state spent plenty of money and resources on getting this conviction, and it's not likely to abandon it on a whim of goodwill."

"I'll keep digging."

"Keep me posted."

Cal hung up and parked along the street in front of the courthouse. Kelly grabbed her gear as the pair got out together.

"What does Marsha Frost think?" Kelly asked.

"She thinks we don't have enough real evidence to get a judge to issue a retrial. We need to find more proof that the defense bungled this case."

Once inside the courthouse, Cal and Kelly obtained permission to sift through the trial transcripts again in the basement archives.

After a few minutes, Kelly shouted aloud. "There you are! I knew I'd seen this before but couldn't remember where or when."

"What'd you find?" Cal asked.

"I thought I remembered reading in the discovery that Susannah's lawyer lover from Jacksonville, Mr. Tanner Thomas, had secured a marriage license two days before her death. That alone was motive enough for Drake to killer her."

"Good point."

Kelly nodded and held up her right index finger. "However, there's something that dawned on me after hearing Mrs. Kirkwood talk at the library: small towns people like to talk."

"*Everyone* likes to talk."

"True. So, based on what Mrs. Kirkwood just told us, aren't there some other questions we should be asking about this case that apparently never got asked."

"Such as . . . ?"

Kelly's eyebrows shot upward, and she broke into a smile. "Such as if Jordan Hayward was upset with Susannah, maybe he found out that she was planning on marrying Tanner Thomas and leaving his buddy Drake in the dust—or himself in the dust."

"Did Drake know about Susannah getting married? Because he certainly didn't mention it when we interviewed him."

"Maybe, maybe not. But if we need hard evidence that creates doubt, this does it."

"Or confirms it. The only way the jury would know is if Hayward or Drake testified to this. Neither of them were on the stand."

"So, how did this information come out in the trial?"

Kelly held up her index finger. "Well, initially it was speculative . . . until this piece of evidence got introduced as 'Exhibit S,' a photograph of the marriage license log from that day."

She handed the picture to Cal.

"What am I looking for here?" Cal asked.

"Check the name of the clerk on the log sheet."

Cal's mouth went agape.

Kelly smiled and nodded. "Now you're tracking with me. The clerk who gave them the marriage license was none other than Heloise Hayward, Jordan's mother."

Cal shrugged. "That still doesn't bolster the level of doubt that Drake did it. If anything, it strengthens it."

"I agree . . . unless the jury didn't know about Hayward's fling with Susannah. And it was never brought up in court."

"Are you suggesting this gives Hayward a motive?"

"Maybe," she said. "A good defense attorney would've brought this information to light in a trial. If anything, they could've hatched a plan together."

Cal nodded knowingly. "Or Hayward was solely responsible."

CHAPTER 19

CAL AWOKE EARLY FRIDAY MORNING and was careful not to wake up Kelly. He took a quick shower and slipped out onto the balcony to enjoy the Okefenokee wildlife just outside his hotel room. After a few days, he was getting acquainted with the various bird calls and other animals communicating throughout the swamp. The serene moments provided him with a chance to clear his head and think about the case.

A man's voice from below jarred Cal, serving as a reminder that his place of zen was shared and unpredictable.

"Sorry I don't have anything to show you from Gus this morning," the man said.

Cal stood up and peered over the balcony at the friendly janitor for the Okefenokee Inn. "That's okay," Cal said. "I'd rather just enjoy the sights and sounds of life than death."

"Death is part of the circle of life," the janitor said. "Don't worry. I'm sure the swamp wasn't all full of peace and harmony last night. Wander around here long enough and you'll see somethin' else dead."

Waving at the man, Cal said, "You have a good day, sir." He retreated inside and found Kelly awake.

"What was that all about?" she asked, squinting as she

looked in his direction.

"Oh, nothing. Just the friendly and morbid Okefenokee Inn grounds keeper."

***

NEVER KNOWN FOR HIS PATIENCE, Cal suggested to Kelly that after breakfast they should visit Heloise Hayward. Cal had learned that she quit working at city hall a few years ago and had taken up as a waitress at a fancy restaurant located near the entrance of the Okefenokee. According to one of the articles he'd read about it, the eatery catered to tourists and didn't open until 11:00 a.m.

"She should still be home if we hustle," Cal said while glancing at his watch.

Kelly agreed, and by 10:00 a.m., they were pulling into Heloise's driveway.

When the car came to a stop and Cal turned it off, his heart-rate quickened at the sound of ferocious barking. He looked up to see a Rottweiler salivating and lunging toward the car. He quickly sighed, relieved once he noticed the chain around the dog's neck.

"Herschel, I done told you a hundred times to treat guests with more respect than that," a woman said as she hobbled down the steps. She grabbed the dog by his collar and held him in place while eyeing Cal and Kelly.

"May I help you?" the woman asked.

Cal approached gingerly, raising his hands in the air in a gesture of surrender.

"Mrs. Hayward?"

"Yes. Who's askin'?"

"I'm Cal Murphy, and this is my wife, Kelly. We're from *The Seattle Times* and working on a story about Isaiah Drake. Would you mind if we asked you a few questions for the article I'm writing?"

She stood up and broke into a wide smile. "As long as you're not from the government, you're welcome. Come on in. Have a seat on the porch while I fetch y'all some sweet tea."

Cal and Kelly sat down on the bench swing and surveyed the surroundings. The clapboard house looked like it had seen better days along with the yard, which was little more than a dirt patch, probably due to Herschel. The only vehicle in the yard was a twenty-year-old BMW that needed a new paint job but otherwise looked like a serviceable vehicle.

The chain link rope attaching the wooden swing to the porch eave creaked as Cal and Kelly shifted on the bench.

"I'm afraid I don't have too much time to talk," Mrs. Hayward said as she returned carrying a platter with three glasses of sweet tea. "I've got to get to work in an hour, but I'll be more than happy to talk with you as long as I can."

She held out the platter in front of Cal and Kelly, waiting for them to take a glass. Once they did, she pulled up a chair from the other side of the porch and sat across from them.

"So, what is a big city paper sending a couple of reporters all the way across the country to little ole Pickett to write about Isaiah Drake for?"

"To be blunt, he's running out of appeals and it looks like his execution might be coming soon," Cal said. "He was a fan favorite in Seattle, and it's been twelve years since the murder of Susannah Sloan."

Mrs. Hayward shook her head. "Mmm, mmm, mmm. That trial tore this town apart. Two of our favorite people in the world. And now they're both gone."

"Both of them were admired?" Kelly asked.

Mrs. Hayward nodded. "That's what made it so painful. We all loved Susannah. She was always smilin' and kind to people. Even when she became the prosecutor, she handled each case with care. Because she knew the families, she understood each one's struggle . . . or lack thereof. Some people needed to get a heavy dose of justice; others just needed mercy and a second chance."

"Like Jordan?" Cal asked.

She nodded emphatically. "Especially Jordan. He was always gettin' into trouble, messin' around with the people he shouldn't have been messin' around with. But he finally got his life straightened out. He's still poor, but at least he ain't gonna die in some drug deal gone wrong."

"And Susannah knew that about him?" Kelly asked.

"Ah, yes. Susannah was an angel. She wanted to see Jordan escape this place."

Cal scooted up on the bench and leaned forward.

"Mrs. Hayward, I hate to ask a question like this, but I was wondering if you knew if Jordan and Susannah were lovers."

"Lovers? Jordan and Susannah? Lawd, no. Whoever told you that has been smokin' crack since Sunday. Those two were just friends, nothin' more."

"Is that why it didn't bother you to issue Susannah and that Jacksonville lawyer Tanner Thomas a marriage license?" Cal asked.

Mrs. Hayward took a deep breath.

"Well, I can't say that didn't bother me. The whole time she was standin' in front of me, I was starin' at that bling on her finger that Isaiah had given her. I was hopin' it might make her reconsider, but it didn't. I thought it was a rotten thing to do, but who am I to judge?"

"When did she come in to get that license?" Kelly asked.

"On Wednesday afternoon, just a couple of days before she was murdered."

"Did you ever share with others about the people who applied for a marriage license?" Cal asked.

Mrs. Hayward chuckled. "Hardly ever. By the time they get to me, it's old news in Pickett County. There's already either been an announcement in the paper or the woman's makin' her own *pronouncement*, if you know what I mean."

Cal and Kelly laughed softly.

"I think I understand," Cal said. "But what about in this case? This would've been different, right? Nobody really knew about Susannah's intent to marry Mr. Thomas until the trial, did they?"

"No, that was the big bombshell in the trial, more than anything. The whole town talked about that excessively after it was over. They just couldn't believe she'd do that to Isaiah after they dated for so long."

"So, Mrs. Hayward, did you tell anyone about that before she died?"

She shook her head. "I don't recollect it."

"Not even your son?" Cal asked, pressing her.

Mrs. Hayward stood up.

"Mr. Murphy, I think it's time you and your wife got goin'. It's gettin' late, and I still gotta finish gettin' ready for work. Have a good day." She stormed inside her house.

Herschel growled from the corner of the yard before the screen door slammed, bouncing several times against the frame before silence fell on the yard.

"Well, I think that went well, didn't it?" Cal asked.

"Let's get out of here before Mrs. Hayward returns," Kelly said.

They hustled down the steps and to their car.

Cal buckled his seatbelt before turning the ignition.

"This story just got a whole lot more interesting, didn't it?"

CHAPTER 20

SATISFIED THAT DRAKE'S LAWYER had failed to provide the football star with a competent defense, Cal wondered aloud if it was time to return to Seattle. With all the interviews they'd conducted and the photos Kelly had snapped, he was confident he could write a compelling story.

But this wasn't just about an assignment for him; this was also about exonerating one of his childhood heroes. Cal quickly decided it wasn't time to leave just yet.

"What did you think about Mrs. Hayward?" Cal asked.

"Based on her response, it's hard to imagine Mrs. Hayward didn't tell her son about the marriage license."

"And if she did tell him—and she was messing around with him—then he'd have the good ole reason of jealousy to kill her."

"But why not kill Thomas?" Kelly countered.

Cal shrugged. "I'm not sure, but maybe he realized he wasn't going to have her no matter what and thought he could get away with it by pinning the murder on Drake."

"That's a good theory," Kelly said. "And that's something a lawyer could make in a retrial that might be more than enough to cause reasonable doubt in the mind of most jurors. I know it's making me doubt everything I've already thought about this case."

As Cal turned back onto Main Street and headed toward Hank's Pawnshop, his phone buzzed. It was Marsha Frost.

"I'm so glad you called, Marsha," Cal said. "Have I got some news for you."

"It's probably nothing compared to the news I just received," she said.

"I'm gonna put you on speaker so Kelly can hear, okay?"

"Okay."

"All right. Fire away. What's happening?"

"I just got a call from Keith Hurley. Name sound familiar to you?"

Cal thought for a moment. "Yes, isn't that the eye witness in the case who said he saw Drake kill Susannah?"

"Bingo. That's the one."

"So, what did he say?"

"He said he made it up. It's all a lie. Somebody told him they'd pay him a thousand bucks to say that he saw Drake kill her. He was just a kid and was out riding his bike around when it happened. He said he never saw anything but jumped at the opportunity to make some quick cash."

"Whoa," Cal said. "Did he know who it was?"

"Said he never saw the guy before, but he was a kid and it was a long time ago. He said it was dark, too, when the man approached him, and he could hardly see his face."

"That changes everything."

"Dang right, it does." She paused. "So, what were you gonna tell me?"

"Does it matter now?"

Frost laughed. "Probably not. I've already contacted one judge, who's supposed to call me back today. If he finds that compelling-enough evidence, he may order a retrial."

"That's great news," Cal said. "What we found out isn't

quite as earth shaking, but it'll help any retrials."

"What'd you find?"

"So, from what we've gathered, Jordan Hayward was also lovers with Susannah Sloan. And Susannah applied for a marriage license with a man named Tanner Thomas just two days before her death. And guess who the clerk at the courthouse was who knew about the marriage license application?"

"Who? The suspense is killing me," Frost said.

"None other than Heloise Hayward, Jordan's mother. And she intimated to us that she told her son about Susannah's intent to marry Mr. Thomas."

"How did Drake's lawyer miss all of this?"

"Your guess is as good as mine. Either way, it's pretty damning as to the incompetency of Sullivan's team running this trial."

"That or either they were way out of their league in the Deep South."

Cal nodded. "That could be it, too. No matter what, do you think that's enough along with Hurley's admission to get a new trial and possibly earn Drake an exoneration?"

"It should be enough . . . and it's definitely enough for us to take the case."

"Excellent!" Cal said. "That's made this entire trip worth it."

"I bet you have one compelling story, too," Frost said.

"I do, but I'm not done yet."

Cal hung up and pulled to a stop just outside Hank's Pawn Shop. He dug into his pocket for a quarter to feed the meter and went inside with Kelly.

"You think Jordan's gonna talk to us now?" Kelly asked in a whisper.

"We'll soon find out." Cal scanned the shop and didn't see anyone inside.

"Hello?" he called.

Moments later, Hank plowed through the swinging double doors that led to the back.

"Can I help you?" Hank said before realizing who was standing in front of him.

"Hello, again. We were wondering if we could speak with Jordan Hayward again," Cal said.

"I wish," Hank growled. "That little lowlife hasn't shown up for work today. So, if you find him, tell him he's late."

"When was the last time you saw him?" Kelly asked.

"He was here yesterday. But he was supposed to be here an hour ago, and I haven't seen hide nor hair of him."

Cal nodded. "Okay. Thanks."

He and Kelly turned toward the door and exited the shop, running right into Crazy Corey Taylor.

"I know who killed Susannah Sloan," Taylor said, bouncing from side to side, while carrying another sign proclaiming the end of days. "Talk to me, and I'll tell you who."

Before Cal could say another word, Hank rushed outside and ran up to Taylor, giving him a swift shove.

"How many times do I have to tell you to get outta here and stop harassing my customers?" Hank said.

"They're not customers," Taylor said.

"Neither are you. Now scram," Hank said.

He turned toward Cal and Kelly as the town's lunatic scampered down the street, lugging his sign behind him.

"I'm really sorry about that," Hank said. "That guy is certifiable, and why he continues to walk the streets of Pickett is one of the world's biggest mysteries if you ask me."

"No harm, no foul," Cal said as he headed toward his car.

"And don't forget—if you see Jordan, tell him he's late for work," Hank said.

Cal raised his hand in acknowledgement without turning around.

Once inside the car, Kelly buckled her seatbelt before asking the obvious question. "Should we go talk to Crazy Corey Taylor?"

"It can't hurt," Cal said. "Plus, it'd add some great color to the story, though Buckman would probably cut it anyway."

"Worth a try," she said.

"You're right. But I want to make a quick visit to the sheriff's office first."

***

ONCE CAL PULLED into a parking spot in front of the Pickett County Sheriff's Office, he realized an unusually large number of people poking their heads inside as well as others milling around outside on the sidewalk.

"What do you think is going on here?" Cal asked before getting out of the car.

"Beats me, but I'd bet it's gonna be good," Kelly said.

They walked up to the crowd and tapped a man on the shoulder.

"What's happening?" Kelly asked him.

"They found a body," he said.

"Where?"

"Somewhere near the swamp."

"Whose is it?" Cal asked.

The man turned to face Cal. "Not sure yet, but I heard it might be Jordan Hayward."

CHAPTER 21

CAL RUSHED BACK to their car and opened up an app on his phone. He needed to see the scene for himself, if for anything to capture it for his article or possibly one that the news side would want. With the likelihood that Isaiah Drake was about to be released, the murder of his best friend from high school on the same day seemed strange and at a minimum newsworthy. But Cal wanted to see the body for himself.

"Are you trying to find out where they are from the scanner?" Kelly asked, following him back to the car.

Cal nodded. "Doesn't it make you miss when we first started out as cub reporters in Statenville?"

"I don't know if *miss* is the word I'd choose, but it definitely makes me sentimental."

Cal searched until he found the Pickett County live feed and listened in. After a few moments of garbled communication and a couple of codes Cal had never heard of, he finally heard that familiar booming voice.

"It's Sheriff Sloan," Kelly said.

"Sshh."

We got a 926 at the north end of Bee Gum Lake, just off Swamp Perimeter Road. Requesting a 901.

"Did you get all of that, Cal?" Kelly asked.

He nodded. "Yep. Buckle up. Let's go."

"Come on. Don't leave me in suspense."

Cal winked at her. "They've got a dead body at the lake, and they need an ambulance."

With the county's law enforcement all working the crime scene, Cal didn't hesitate to stomp on the accelerator once they left the city limits. Their twenty-mile trip took only fifteen minutes. And when they pulled up to the scene, Cal was amazed that *The Searchlight's* editor Larry Arant was already there.

"Nothing gets by ole Larry, does it?" Cal asked Kelly.

"Speaking of getting by, I'm not sure we're going to be able to get by one of Sheriff Sloan's deputies."

She nodded in the direction of a deputy Cal didn't recognize. The deputy was placing sawhorses every few feet to create a crime scene around the perimeter. Cal noted that most of the people at the scene were first responders, though he saw a few Looky-Lous wander up to find out what was going on. Cal thought the saw horses were a bit of an overkill.

"What's next? Helicopters overhead to keep the news choppers from getting footage for the six o'clock news?" Cal asked.

"You'll have to ask Arant if this is protocol for Pickett County. Maybe it is."

"Don't make me laugh," Cal said dryly.

"Turn around," Kelly said, nodding to Cal's right. "Here's your chance to find out."

Cal spun to see Larry Arant shuffling toward him.

"Larry," Cal said as he offered his hand, "it's so good to see you. You made it out here quickly, didn't you?"

Arant nodded imperceptibly. "Murders around here happen about as often as a day in July without gnats. Gotta enjoy 'em while you can." He patted his pants pocket. "Those scanner apps are somethin' else, aren't they?"

"Have Sheriff Sloan or any of his deputies let you know what's going on yet?" Cal asked.

"Not yet."

"So, they're keeping you in the dark?"

Arant started laughing before he broke into a coughing fit. Once he stopped, he continued. "Sloan's boys live in the dark. If Isaiah Drake had woken up in that boat without a soul around him, I'm not sure he would've ever been tied to Susannah's murder all those years ago. Aside from Deputy Tillman, these Pickett County deputies make Barney Fife seem like Sherlock Holmes. And I say that as someone whose cousin works for the department."

"Is your cousin working the case?" Cal asked.

"Who? My cousin Betty? She's lucky if she can find her way out of bed in the mornin'."

Cal wasn't sure if he should laugh or not, deciding to go with a forced smile. He craned his neck around Arant to see a large figure coming toward them. It was Sheriff Sloan.

"You mind givin' me a statement?" Arant asked as Sloan approached them.

Sloan stopped and exhaled. He glanced at his watch and looked back at the scene. "Not at this time, gentleman . . . and lady," Sloan said. "We still have to sort through this scene, so I'm afraid I wouldn't be much help anyway."

Cal furrowed his brow. "Can you at least give us the victim's name?"

"Not until we can confirm his identity," Sloan answered.

"So, it's a male?" Cal asked again.

"It's a dead person, Mr. Murphy," Sloan said, his gaze bouncing back and forth between Cal and Kelly. "Didn't I tell y'all it was time to get out of town?"

Cal nodded.

"He's not very good at following directions," Kelly said, throwing her hands in the air. "I ought to know—I live with the man. If I've asked him once to pick up his dirty clothes in the bathroom, I've asked him a thousand—"

Sloan narrowed his eyes. "The last thing Pickett wants is another media frenzy descending on our little town, so I strongly suggest you skedaddle back to Seattle and let the local newspaper editor here handle the story."

"Do you have a suspect in custody?" Cal asked.

"I'm beginnin' to get concerned about your hearin', Mr. Murphy," Sloan said. "It seems like you're havin' a hard time with it. So, I'm going to say this again slowly and loudly: Get out of my town, and don't come back."

Cal remained undaunted. "Why? Afraid of what little secrets I might unearth about you? Scared I might tell Larry here about how you covered up the fact that you were out of the office the night of Susannah's murder at the exact time of her death?"

Larry's eyes bulged out as his mouth fell agape. "Sheriff, is that true?"

Sloan waved dismissively at Arant but maintained his steely gaze on Cal. "Better stop talkin', son, before you dig yourself a hole that you can't climb out of."

Cal fished his recorder out of his pocket and dangled the device in front of Sloan's face. "I hope nothing happens to me because this conversation will be challenging to explain."

Sloan spun around and stormed off in a huff.

Arant watched the sheriff for a few moments before turning back to Cal and Kelly. "I've rarely seen him that rattled," Arant said. "Usually, he's so even keel."

"That's not the Sheriff Sloan we've come to know and love," Cal said.

"Yeah, he's been on edge since we came to town," Kelly added. "What could possibly be bothering him?"

"Aside from you two picking at the old wounds this story conjures up for people around here? I'm sure he would've preferred to leave it buried along with Susannah all those years ago."

"Wait," Cal began. "You aren't the least bit curious about what we found out about the night of Susannah's murder?"

"I am," Arant said. "I'm not gonna lie. I'm a journalist. But I'm also a small town journalist. I live with these people, and I have to get along with them. If I wrote about every secret I knew about and put it on the front page of *The Searchlight*, I'd hardly have a friend left, much less any subscribers."

"But this is *murder*," Cal said. "And it's being pinned on a guy who might be getting executed very soon for something he didn't do. If there was ever a time to cast aside your neighborly approach when it comes to running your paper, this is it."

"You don't live here, Mr. Murphy, so I don't expect you to understand."

"You're right. I don't live here. But I do have some level of expectation of you as a journalist when it pertains to something as serious as this. This town needs to know about this. Everybody needs to know about it."

Arant took a deep breath and exhaled slowly. He stared off at the scene behind Cal as an ambulance pulled up next to the blockade before it was allowed inside the perimeter.

"What if I told you things aren't always as they seem?" Arant asked. "Appearances can be deceiving. Maybe he has a good reason for not wanting that information to get out."

"Yeah, like he *murdered* someone and tried to cover it up," Cal said, his voice rising with each exchange.

Arant held up his hands in a gesture of surrender. "Look, I know what this may look like to you, but I've known Sheriff Sloan for a long time, and he's never shown even an inkling that he might have violent tendencies. He's a gentle giant. Add that to the fact that he was always doting on Susannah, I just can't see him having the gumption to murder his own child like that."

Cal shook his head in disbelief. "Would you have thought that about Isaiah Drake if the roles were reversed? Would you believe that he could've killed Susannah either?"

Arant remained pensive for a few seconds, crossing his arms before looking down at the dirt. He kicked at a rock with his foot. "I wouldn't have predicted him doing something like that, but I can't say I was completely surprised."

Cal's eyebrows shot up. He glanced at Kelly, whose expression matched his own.

"And why would you say you weren't completely surprised?" Cal asked.

Before Arant answered, a couple of black Suburbans screeched to a halt near the crime scene, knocking down the sawhorses.

"What the—?" Arant muttered, ignoring Cal and walking toward the scene.

Cal turned around to see what he figured to be several federal agents hustling toward Sheriff Sloan and the dead body being hoisted onto a stretcher by a pair of EMTs.

The trio of journalists watched from afar as the conversation between the feds and Sloan involved plenty of animation. Finger wagging, throwing hands in the air, kicking at the dirt—Sloan looked like a baseball manager getting in his last two cents with an umpire after getting ejected from a game.

"What do you reckon that's all about?" Arant wondered aloud.

"Is this part of the Okefenokee protected by the federal government?" Cal asked.

Arant shrugged. "Depends on where they found the body. Portions of Bee Gum Lake are, but not all of it. Why does that matter?"

"Jurisdiction. If it's a national forest or reserve, the feds take over the investigation. Otherwise, it's a local matter."

"But how'd the feds get here so fast?" Arant asked.

"Now, that's a really good question," Cal said. "Maybe we can ask Sheriff Sloan when he comes over here."

"Screw 'em," Sloan yelled as he stormed toward the journalists.

"What is it, Sheriff?" Arant asked.

"The damn feds are comin' in here and takin' over my case," Sloan said, breaking into jittery nervous laughter. "And they told me not to tell you a thing. Well, I say *screw 'em*. I'll even tell you, Mr. Hot Shot reporter," he said as he looked at Cal.

"What can you tell us at this time, Sheriff?" Arant asked.

"The deceased is Jordan Hayward. He was found lying dead in a johnboat with a gun in his hand. It looked like a staged suicide to me."

"Just to be clear, as a source close to the investigation," Cal said with a reassuring wink, "you're of the opinion that it wasn't a suicide? And his body was found in a johnboat?"

"That's right on both accounts. Somebody wanted us to think it was suicide."

Cal shook his head. "Sounds eerily familiar to how your deputy found Isaiah Drake all those years ago."

Sloan nodded and complained for another few minutes about the feds taking over his murder case.

Cal was listening so intently that he didn't see Kelly slip off. After a few minutes, he noticed she was missing and scanned the area to locate her. When he finally did, he watched her click off a few photos.

She's always thinking. Man, I love that woman.

When Sloan finished ranting, he stormed toward his truck. In an apparent rush to leave, dirt and rocks flew everywhere as Sloan's vehicle roared away from the crime scene.

"Well, that was interesting," Cal said. "Let's go introduce ourselves to the feds."

Arant declined and headed straight for his car.

Cal shook a couple of the agents' hands, but they all stonewalled him just like he knew they would.

Doesn't hurt to try.

Cal hustled back to his car, where Kelly was waiting for him. She grinned wide and motioned hurriedly for him to join her.

"What is it?" Cal asked as he got inside the car.

"I decided to take some pictures of the scene, as I'm sure *The Times* would want them to go along with your story," she said.

"Good thinking, honey. I can always count on you to be two steps ahead."

"No, that's not the good part. It's when I started taking pictures, I caught someone lurking in the shadows near the tree line."

She held out her camera and showed the display screen to Cal.

"Now, who does that look like to you?" she asked.

"I can't quite tell on this small image area. Can you put it on your computer for me?"

"Give me a minute," Kelly said as she took the camera from Cal's hands. She worked quickly to retrieve the memory card and then placed it in a slot on her laptop. The computer whirred and came to life as it downloaded the photos.

After a few more seconds, she turned the screen around to Cal.

Cal stared at the screen again, glaring hard at it.

"Is that who I think it is?" he asked.

Kelly nodded. "Yep. None other than Jacob Boone."

CHAPTER 22

CAL AND KELLY DECIDED to grab a quick bite to eat at Curly's Diner for a late lunch. He figured the lunchtime crowd would be cleared out—but he was wrong. They managed to snag the only available table as it seemed as though the entire town descended upon the popular eatery to put their heads together as to who killed Jordan Hayward.

Curly hustled over to Cal and Kelly's table.

"You two know how to stir things up," Curly said with a wink.

"Don't blame me," Cal said. "We're just here to get a good story."

"Now you're going to get a better one than you bargained for, aren't you?"

Cal grinned. "All we need now is for the Marsh Monster to make an appearance on Main Street."

Curly wagged his finger at Cal. "Don't laugh. The Marsh Monster is in a dead heat for first when it comes to identifying a suspect. To the people around here, that monster is no joking matter."

"So, what humans made the list of suspects?" Kelly asked.

"You wouldn't recognize most of the names since Jordan Hayward was a known drug dealer."

154 | R.J. PATTERSON

Cal cocked his head and stared at Curly.

"Hayward is a known drug dealer? How come Sheriff Sloan hasn't done anything to him?"

"Oh, he has, plenty of times. Hayward's been in and out of jail for drugs, but the charges don't always stick or they just dismiss them for various and odd reasons. It's probably been about five years since he was last arrested. He was still dealing, but most people suspect he and the Sheriff came to some kind of an understanding."

"What kind?" Kelly asked.

"The kind where the Sheriff leaves Hayward alone, probably in exchange for a hefty donation to the department."

"So, maybe he missed a payment?" Cal suggested.

Curly shrugged. "Maybe. If the first part of that hypothesis is true, that would certainly be a logical conclusion."

"Who else makes the list?" Kelly asked.

"Patrick Simmons, one of the drug runners from Hayward's crew. Jacob Boone, who was routinely seen arguing with Hayward. Most people think Boone and Hayward were always up to something. Also, there's some talk about how fast Sheriff Sloan arrived at the scene and how fishy that seems."

"Wild theories abound," Cal said.

"Yes, they do," Curly said. "And let's not forget that Manley's Department Store across the street sells fitted tin-foil hats . . . and he's always running out."

"What's your best guess?" Kelly asked.

"The Marsh Monster, hands down. Now, enough of that. Can I take your order?"

Cal and Kelly ordered their meals and didn't have time to discuss anything else before Larry Arant strode through the front door. Without an available seat, he shuffled over toward Cal and Kelly's table.

"Mind if I join you?" Arant asked.

"Are you sure you want to?" Cal asked.

Arant nodded. "I'd spend the rest of my lunch answering questions about the case if I sat with anyone else."

Cal chuckled. "What do you think *we're* going to talk about?"

"Well, at least you won't be pitching me cockamamie theories and asking me to agree with you or worse—print them."

"Good point."

Curly dropped off Cal and Kelly's sweet teas before quickly taking Arant's order and vanishing into the kitchen.

"Now, you said back at the lake that you wouldn't have predicted Drake committing murder but that it didn't completely surprise you either. Care to elaborate? Is there something we don't know about?"

Arant shifted in his seat and leaned forward, resting his elbows on the table. He glanced around the room before he began speaking in a hushed tone. "What I'm about to tell you I'm doing so in the strictest of confidence," Arant began. "And I'm doing this because I want you to get a full picture of who Isaiah Drake is—or at least, was."

"Go on," Cal said, leaning in closer.

"When Drake was a freshman in high school, he was with two other boys who beat and robbed an elderly woman. They put her in the hospital, all for fifty bucks. Sheriff Sloan tracked down the trio. Only one of the boys was punished with a short stint in a juvenile detention center."

"Who were the other two boys?"

Arant shrugged. "I could guess, but nobody really knows, so that wouldn't be fair."

"Then how do you know about Drake?" Kelly asked.

"One night I was at The Pirate's Den having a couple of drinks with Sheriff Sloan, and he told me the story. He said he let Drake go partly because he wasn't convinced he was a participant in the attack. The Sheriff also said he saw how much potential Drake had on the football field and hoped to steer him to Auburn. So, when I say I wasn't surprised that Drake was capable of such a thing, that's why."

"Because he allegedly beat up a little old lady?" Cal asked. "That's quite a leap from there to being a killer."

"Anyone who beats up an elderly person has something wrong with them."

"Allegedly," Kelly added. "He *allegedly* beat her up with two other men."

"I never wrote that nor did I ever tell anyone. But just know that Drake isn't a saint."

Cal nodded. "Hayward was my prime suspect in the murder of Susannah Sloan, but not anymore. Now, I'm baffled by it all. Okay, so answer me this: Who do you think killed Jordan Hayward?"

Arant leaned back in his seat and glanced around the room. "Same person who I think killed Susannah Sloan—it was Isaiah Drake."

CHAPTER 23

MRS. LOUISE KIRKWOOD SAT UP STRAIGHT, fingers interlocked and resting on the desk in front of her at her station in the Pickett County Library reference section. Cal thought he detected a faint smile on her face the moment he and Kelly walked into her line of sight.

"Back to solve some more mysteries?" Mrs. Kirkwood asked, clapping her hands quietly.

"We're trying," Kelly said.

"Yes, and we were hoping you might be able to help us some more," Cal added.

Mrs. Kirkwood stood up. "Give me a moment while I lock up my desk, and I'll meet you back in the microfiche room."

Cal and Kelly followed Mrs. Kirkwood's instructions and waited for her, spending their time discussing how Drake could have orchestrated a hit on Jordan Hayward from prison.

"It just doesn't make sense," Cal said. "Why wait all this time? If you had the resources to kill Hayward, why not do it years ago? The timing of it all makes me want to dismiss that theory altogether."

"Let me play devil's advocate for a moment," Kelly said,

holding up her index finger. "What if Drake took all this time to figure out a way to get the state's major eyewitness to recant . . . and now Drake needs to make sure nobody else talks or jeopardizes his chances at getting cleared in a retrial?"

"That's an interesting theory, though when we talked with him, I never detected any animosity from Drake regarding his childhood best friend."

"Psychopaths are good at hiding things."

Cal's eyes widened. "So you think Drake is a psychopath now?"

"Remember, I'm just being the devil's advocate. If you're going to write a comprehensive feature on this story, you need to consider all the possibilities."

"I'm having a hard time seeing that."

"All I'm saying is it could be true. Just think about it."

Before Cal could ponder Kelly's theory any further, the door clicked open and Mrs. Kirkwood entered.

"So, what is it I get the pleasure of helping you with today?" she asked.

"I just want to say first that we appreciate your willingness to help us again," Cal said. "You have no idea how difficult it is for us to piece this story together as outsiders."

Mrs. Kirkwood snickered.

"What's so amusing?" Kelly asked.

"Oh, you two think it's difficult to delve into the dark secrets and hidden motivations of Pickett County residents as outsiders? I think it's far more difficult to do that as an insider. It's hard to get your preconceived ideas, notions, and history about your neighbors out of the way."

"When you put it that way, I tend to agree with you," Cal said. "I've lived and worked in a small town before. It certainly has its unique challenges, especially when it comes to privacy."

Mrs. Kirkwood raised her right hand in the air. "Amen to that, brother," she said. "Now, what can I help y'all find?"

She clicked on the microfiche machine as the light flickered and the cooling fan whirred to life.

"We want to read up about Jacob Boone and find out about his criminal past—or professional one," Cal said.

Mrs. Kirkwood marched over to the filing cabinet and pulled out one of the sheets. "This won't be difficult," she said. "He had a case that was a big deal around here at the time. It really divided the community."

"How so?" Kelly asked.

Mrs. Kirkwood slid the microfiche sheet into place as she talked. "In February of 2003, Jacob Boone was arrested for possession of meth with intent to distribute. He was facing hefty jail time. He claimed that he was set up, but he looked the part of a junky. He lived in a run-down trailer on the outskirts of town with his two kids, who were ages five and seven at the time. His wife died of an overdose a year after their youngest was born. He struggled to hold a job but wasn't on welfare as far as anyone knew, so the prevailing assumption was that he ran drugs to pay the bills. I don't like to engage in such gossip, but that was how most people viewed him . . . and it certainly made sense."

"What happened in the trial?" Cal asked.

Mrs. Kirkwood pointed at the screen and stood up, offering the seat to Cal. "As you'll read, it was a lengthy trial and full of emotion," she said. "One of the biggest reasons why Jacob was so upset was because he would lose his children to the foster care system if he went to prison. There were no fit relatives to take the kids, and with a father in prison on drug charges, it was unlikely he'd ever get the chance to get them back."

"And how might this be tied to Susannah Sloan?" Kelly asked.

"Susannah was the prosecutor in the case and showed no mercy in what the state was asking for at sentencing— fourteen years. However, the judge showed leniency and sentenced him to seven years. However, he was released after three months for good behavior. Yet the damage was already done when it came to his kids, who became wards of the state. After he came back, he turned into an even more bitter person, as if that was even possible after his wife died. It was just sad to watch."

"Has anyone spoken with him about it since?" Cal asked.

"A few people here and there. He still maintains his innocence, but I think everyone in town knows he's still dealing drugs. Why Sheriff Sloan hasn't arrested him again is beyond me."

Cal scanned the article by Larry Arant about the trial, confirming everything Mrs. Kirkwood said. "It blows my mind that no one investigated him as a person of interest in Susannah Sloan's death," he said. "Jacob Boone was released from prison just a few months before her murder. Seems like he'd be a good candidate to murder her."

"Perhaps you're right, but everyone around Pickett trusts Sheriff Sloan implicitly," Mrs. Kirkwood said. "Well . . . almost everyone. Every sheriff has detractors."

Cal stood up and offered his hand to Mrs. Kirkwood.

"Thank you for your help, ma'am," he said. "You've proven to be most helpful, and don't be surprised if we pop in here again before we leave."

Mrs. Kirkwood shook Cal's hand and then Kelly's.

"It's my pleasure. Always a joy to help people." Mrs. Kirkwood gestured toward the door. "Let me walk you out."

Cal and Kelly followed Mrs. Kirkwood through the double glass doors and onto the sidewalk in front of the library. As soon as they all stepped into the warm sun, Mrs. Kirkwood's mouth fell agape as she watched a BMW roll by on the street.

"You like that car?" Cal asked, grinning as Mrs. Kirkwood continued to gawk. "I don't think I would've pegged you for a car person."

She turned slowly toward Cal. "I'm not, but I know that's a nice automobile . . . and Keith Hurley is the one driving it."

Kelly whipped her head in Mrs. Kirkwood's direction. "Did you say, *Keith Hurley*?"

"Sure did," Mrs. Kirkwood replied. "I know he's not making enough working at Ludwig's Tires to afford that car. Look at it—brand spankin' new." She turned back toward the library. "Y'all have a good day now, okay?"

Cal and Kelly waved at her as she returned inside. He was thinking something, but Kelly said it out loud.

"Renounces his testimony, gets a high-end foreign car. Makes sense to me," she said.

"Let's not jump to conclusions," Cal said. "Besides, we've got enough suspects to vet before I write this article. Let's not add any more."

"Why not? It'll just be that much more of a better story."

Cal sighed and shook his head slowly. "I don't know about you, but I'd like to leave this town before we start getting our mail at the Okefenokee Inn and little Maddie forgets what we look like."

Kelly hung her head. "You just had to mention Maddie, didn't you?"

Cal nodded. "You should call her." He checked his watch. "She should be getting out of her preschool class about now."

Kelly pulled out her phone and started to dial her sister's number. However, an elderly woman interrupted Kelly, and she froze.

"Are y'all the ones writin' for a big newspaper and investigatin' the murder of Ms. Susannah Sloan?" the woman asked.

Cal and Kelly both turned around to see a woman hobbling on a walker toward them.

"Yes, ma'am, we sure are," Cal said. "Can we help you?"

"I hope so," she said. "My name is Gertie Rollins, and there's somethin' I've been wantin' to get off my chest for quite a while now."

"And how can we help you do that, Ms. Rollins?" Kelly asked.

"I saw Sheriff Sloan at his daughter's house the night she was murdered right around the time she supposedly died."

CHAPTER 24

CAL OFFERED HIS ARM to Gertie as he and Kelly led the woman across the street to a small park. They helped her onto a bench in the shade and sat down on opposite sides of her. Gertie leaned forward on her walker, adjusting her position until she appeared comfortable.

"We'd love to hear your story, Ms. Rollins," Cal said. "How come you never told anyone about this before now?"

"Oh, I did. Believe you me. I told anyone who would listen, but everyone just laughed at me. They said I needed to change my prescription," Gertie said, grabbing her bottle-thick glasses for emphasis. "They told me I was too blind, or it was too dark, or I was just lookin' for my fifteen minutes of fame. I finally just gave up on it all."

"You apparently haven't given up on it if you're telling us," Kelly said, patting the woman on her back.

Gertie chuckled, flashing a toothy grin. "I guess you're right."

"So, tell us what you saw," Cal said, pulling out his notebook and voice recorder. "You don't mind if I record this, do you?"

"Please do," Gertie said. "That way if anything happens to me, at least you'll have a record of it that no one can deny."

"Excellent. Please proceed," Cal said, turning on his recorder.

"Well, the night that Susannah Sloan was murdered, I was out for a bike ride. I wasn't always like this," she said, gesturing to her feet and walker. "I used to enter every 5K in South Georgia until I needed a hip replacement about five years ago. I was in so much pain, I could barely stand. I digress. Anyway, I was out for a late evening bike ride and returned home around 9:30. I barely had enough fireflies to light my way home, but the street lights helped, too. After I put my bike up, I walked around to the front of my house to sit on my bench on the front porch and read. But when I sat down, I looked out across the way at Susannah Sloan's place, which was right across the street from me, and watched Sheriff Sloan pull into her driveway."

"About what time was this?" Cal asked.

"Somewhere around quarter to ten."

"And you knew it was him how?"

"There aren't many strapping men in Pickett County like Sheriff Sloan," Gertie said, her cheeks turning a light shade of red. "There are some big men around here; don't get me wrong. But most of them don't have his physique. Well, at least the physique he had about twelve years ago."

"Okay," Cal said. "Go on."

"Anyway, I thought it was odd of him to stop by so late on a Friday night. I still ascribe to the neighborhood watch philosophy and am always looking out my window to see if anything is going on, strange noises, tires screeching, and what not. And when the weather warms up, I used to always ride my bike every evening around that time, so I would've known what was going on and typical patterns."

"What struck you as odd that night?" Kelly asked.

"Two things did. The first one was that Susannah was at home. She usually was out of town or out for the evening by 9:30 on a Friday evening. At least two weekends out of the month, she went out of town. And I know this because she used to ask me to feed her dog, a little Pomeranian named Fitz. Susannah rarely had visitors."

"And her father never dropped by?" Cal asked.

"He would occasionally, but never that late and never on a Friday night. At the time, I noted it was strange behavior on both their parts, but I didn't give it a second thought . . . until she wound up murdered the next morning."

"And everyone refused to listen to your story?" Cal asked.

"Yes, and I mean I can't really blame them. Nobody around here would ever believe Sheriff Sloan would be capable of killing his own daughter, myself included. But after I saw him there that night, I believe it's possible he did it."

"Proving that is going to be very difficult since he oversaw the investigation. I'll consider all these things as I'm writing my story."

"You know what another strange thing is?" Gertie asked.

"What's that?" Cal asked.

"The Pickett County Sheriff's Department had relatively no turnover for dang near twenty years. But after this happened, I think almost every deputy moved, transferred, or was fired within a year."

"And nobody in the community thought that was odd?" Kelly asked.

"I think everybody thought it was strange but just attributed it to the fact that a meaner and grieving sheriff emerged from all that. Sheriff Sloan used to be far more kind and compassionate than he is now. Understandably so, this whole event changed his life. It took away the only remaining woman in his life that he loved. He pretty much became a bitter and hardened man."

"Well, if he actually did kill his own daughter, that'd definitely change him," Kelly said.

"So, do you believe me?" Gertie asked.

Cal and Kelly both nodded.

"We hear you and believe you could be right," Cal said.

"Well, that's a first," she said.

"I'm not sure if I believe *he* killed her though."

Gertie waved him off dismissively.

"I'm not so concerned about that. I can't be a hundred percent sure about that. But as long as you believe I'm telling you the truth, I'm satisfied. I got it off my chest, and you can do with that information whatever you want. It's in your hands now … and on *your* conscience."

Cal stood and offered a hand to Gertie, assisting her to stand. She put both her hands on her walker and started to shuffle off.

"Thank you for listenin'," she said.

"What do you make of that?" Kelly asked after Gertie was out of earshot.

Cal shrugged. "Just more work for us. We're far from being done here."

CHAPTER 25

"CHANGE OF PLANS," Cal said once he and Kelly got into their car. "I think we need to get everything we can out of Sheriff Sloan for this story before we question him directly about Ms. Rollins' claim that he visited Susannah during the time she was believed to be murdered."

Kelly agreed, and they drove the short distance to the Pickett County Sheriff's Department.

Once they entered the office, Cal figured he might only be going to get one more shot at Sloan. When conducting an interview of a particularly accusatory nature, Cal understood how to negotiate the conversation in a way so he could emerge with good quotes for his story before he got cursed out. For him, this skill required patience and taking advantage of any goodwill he'd acquired. In this instance, Cal had no goodwill, but Sloan had plenty of ill will for the government—and Cal knew how to leverage it.

"Betty, is Sheriff Sloan around?" Cal asked.

Betty rolled her eyes and huffed. Cal could tell she was tired of seeing them, though he wasn't sure if it had more to do with how Sloan acted after they left or how she held a general disdain for reporters snooping around. However, she clearly wasn't in a fighting mood. Betty opened the door to the office area and gestured for Cal and Kelly to enter—all while never uttering a word.

Cal and Kelly wove through a handful of desks until they reached the back of the room where Sloan was. He was muttering something to himself and pounding away on his keyboard with his index fingers. Cal guessed Sloan was likely writing a letter to some federal agent's superior about how the sheriff was mistreated. Or perhaps it was an email complaining about his loss of jurisdiction in the case. Regardless of whoever was on the receiving end of Sloan's wrath, Cal figured they would likely ignore the note and file it in the trash. Cal would've preferred to encounter Sloan when he wasn't in such an angry disposition, but Cal recognized that the silver lining was that the sheriff's ire was directed at someone else. And at the moment, it was as good as Cal could hope to get.

Cal knocked on the door jamb of Sloan's office. Sloan didn't look up.

"What is it?" he groused.

"Sheriff, mind if we have a quick word with you?" Cal asked.

Sloan stopped typing and turned around in his chair to face Cal and Kelly. "Didn't I give you what you wanted at the lake?"

He spun back around in his chair and continued typing.

"We have a few more questions for you, if you don't mind," Cal said.

"Well, I do mind. I'm very busy right now."

"What? Typing a letter that someone is going to throw away seconds after reading it?"

Sloan slammed both his fists on his desk at the same time before letting out an exasperated growl. "You're probably right … for once," Sloan said, slowly turning back around to face his visitors. "What do you want to know?"

Cal looked down at his notepad. "Was there a weapon found at the crime scene for Jordan Hayward?"

Sloan shook his head. "The murder was likely committed somewhere else, which is why I'm pretty pissed about the feds sweeping in and taking the body."

"Was it a gunshot wound? A knife wound? What killed him?"

"Obviously I don't have a coroner's report, but based on the bruising around his neck and the lack of any other type of visible wound, I would guess cause of death will be asphyxiation."

Cal took a deep breath before launching into his next question. "Could this murder have been committed by the same person who killed your daughter?"

Sloan scowled. "What the hell kind of question is that? You know Isaiah Drake is still in jail and may that bastard rot there. So to answer your asinine question, *no*."

Cal flipped through a few pages in his notes. He wasn't looking for anything in particular but was mentally preparing himself for the best way to ask his next question, the kind of question that would turn the conversation from tense to a full-fledged storm of wrath and fury. "Sheriff, one last question before we leave and get out of your hair for good."

"Thank God," Sloan said. "I'll answer anything to get rid of you two."

"So, the night that Susannah was murdered, where did you go when you left the office?"

A wry grin spread across Sloan's face. "I thought we already went through this. I was here all night."

"The records you let us go through when we got here—

we saw where you logged out between 9:30 p.m. and 11:00 p.m. Where did you go?"

"These logs?" Sloan said as he pointed at a log book on his desk.

Cal nodded. "That's the one."

"This log?" Sloan asked again, his tone almost mocking Cal.

"Would you mind turning to the page with the date of May 7, 2004?"

Sloan opened the book and began turning the pages. When he arrived at the page, he stopped and smiled. "Well, would you look at that? I didn't log out that night. Y'all must've been lookin' at the wrong book."

"Let me see that," Cal said as both he and Kelly leaned down close to study the log book after Sloan held it out to them.

Sloan stood up. "Do you see it now? You must've made a mistake when you first reviewed it. Mistakes happen. All is forgiven, especially if you get the hell out of my town now and never come back."

Kelly narrowed her eyes. "Good thing I took a picture of the log book before you doctored it."

"Doctored it?" Sloan said. "You think I doctored something? Well, good luck with that one. You say *I* doctored it; I say *you* are full of it. Nobody's gonna believe your photoshopped picture of my log anyway."

Cal backed away from the desk, holding his recorder out so that it would capture more clearly anything Sloan said.

"Maybe not," Cal said, "but I'll bet they'll believe a witness who told me that she saw you at your daughter's house around the time of Susannah's death."

"I hope you're not insinuating what I think you are," Sloan said. He then pointed to the door. "Out now! And don't come back!"

CHAPTER 26

CAL GRABBED THE BELL before it clanked against the glass as he and Kelly entered Hank's Pawn Shop. Cal expected a somber environment since he was sure that the news of Jordan Hayward's death had already spread like wildfire in the tight-knit community. But he didn't expect to find an empty showroom again.

"Hello?" Cal called. "Is anyone here?"

He waited a beat. Nothing.

"Hello?" Kelly said. "Anybody home?"

Except for the faint sound of a radio playing from somewhere else in the building, it was eerily silent.

"Let's go find out what's going on," Cal said, pressing ahead toward the doorway to the back. He parted the thick plastic strips hanging over the doorjamb and held them open for Kelly. Once she walked through, he turned to see Hank staring at a chest full of money.

Hank looked up at the pair after Cal cleared his throat.

"This isn't what it looks like, I swear," Hank said, a cigarette bobbing as it dangled from his lips. He stood up and stepped back from a large wooden trunk, a trunk loaded with neat stacks of twenty-dollar bills.

Cal noticed the name Jordan etched into the side of the box and a crowbar lying next to it.

172 | R.J. PATTERSON

"I'm not the cops, Hank, so you don't have to worry about me," Cal said. "But this does raise some suspicion about what you're doing right now with presumably Jordan's chest, which is full of money."

Hank used his foot to flip the lid shut before resting his right leg on top of the chest.

"I'm not sure I know what you're talking about," Hank said, glancing down at the crowbar.

Cal eyed Hank closely and waited a second. In a flash, Cal jammed his foot on top of the bar, raking it to himself along the concrete floor. It wasn't a moment too soon, either, as Hank had lunged for the prying device as well.

Cal held his hands up in a posture of surrender.

"We just came here to talk about Jordan Hayward's death and see if you guys know anything," Cal said. "We don't want any trouble."

"And neither do we. So, I suggest you get on outta here."

Kelly perked up. "Without any answers? I don't think so."

One of Hank's employees, who'd been watching the entire exchange take place from a corner of the room, stepped forward. He had the name Gary emblazoned on an oval name tag attached to the right side of his chest.

"Jordan was into some—"

Hank held up his hand. "What's wrong with you, Gary? Do you wanna get killed, too?"

"No, sir, I don't. That's why I think you oughta tell them—"

Hank spun around and started yelling over him. "Another word out of you and you're fired. You understand me?"

Gary nodded and continued sifting through a pile of musical instruments scattered haphazardly on a storage shelf.

Hank turned back around to face Cal and Kelly.

"I'm not sure how Jordan got all this money. It certainly is odd that he'd wanna keep it here at work."

Gary rattled around with the instruments, making plenty of noise.

"You sure he wasn't stealing from you?" Cal asked.

"I keep the books myself, so I'd know if he was," Hank said. "Wherever this came from, it wasn't this store."

Gary stood up and jogged toward them. "Stop lying through your teeth, Hank, and tell them the truth. At least maybe Jordan will get some justice. He's dead now. It's the least he deserves."

Hank sneered. "Jordan deserved a bullet to the head."

"That's not how it ended for him," Cal said.

"Oh?" Hank said, somewhat surprised.

"Strangled to death, likely by someone he knew."

"Tell 'em, Hank."

"Shut up, Gary," Hank said.

Gary strode toward the trio, refusing to comply with Hank's demands to be quiet.

"It was the Enforcer."

"The *who?*" Kelly asked.

Hank put his hand on his forehead, shaking it as he glowered at Gary in disgust.

"I told you not to say another word," Hank said.

Gary ignored Hank and continued to answer Cal. "Jordan worked for a regional drug dealer named the Enforcer. The word on the street was the Enforcer was looking for Jordan because he was supposedly skimming some money off the top. Needless to say, you don't wanna mess with the Enforcer."

"So, you don't think any of this had to do with Isaiah Drake's case?"

Gary furrowed his brow, staring awkwardly at Cal. "Why would it?"

Cal shrugged. "Just a theory I'm playing with."

"Uh, no. Jordan had plenty of problems, but he and Drake were thick as thieves, literally."

"Literally?" Kelly asked. "Meaning, they were actually thieves?"

Gary nodded. "Not sure about Jordan, but I know Drake got caught once with some other guys. I can't remember who all was involved, but I know the sheriff let Drake off the hook."

"Gary, you're gonna get popped in the mouth if you keep talkin'," Hank groused. "Especially if you keep talkin' about things that you don't really know about."

Cal cocked his head and stared at Hank. "So, since you obviously know what happened, do you want to tell me?"

Hank glared at Gary. "I think Gary has said enough for the both of us."

"Suit yourself," Cal said. "I won't ever reveal you as my source if you change your mind." He handed Hank a business card. "Call me if you decide you want to help me tell an authentic story."

Hank snatched the card from Cal's hand and shuffled off toward his office.

Cal turned to Gary. "Thanks. I appreciate all your help."

"Good luck, y'all," Gary said.

"Keep your luck," Kelly said over her shoulder as she and Cal began walking away. "Based on how your boss just responded, you'll probably be needing it more than we will."

Cal and Kelly returned to the Okefenokee Inn so Cal could write his story about the mysterious circumstances surrounding Jordan Hayward's death and Kelly could upload a few pictures. In about an hour, they were both done and determined a celebration was in order at The Pirate's Den later that evening.

Just as they were about to walk out the door, Cal's cell rang. It was Marsha Frost.

"I was just thinking about calling you," Cal said. "This story just keeps getting better and better. It shouldn't be too long before I have enough solid evidence to help exonerate Isaiah Drake. Not even a recent law school graduate could whiff on this case."

"Better hurry," Frost said. "I just received a phone call from one of the judges handling Drake's case, informing me that Drake was just denied a retrial and for now remains locked up."

"What? Are you kidding me?" Cal said. "How could they possibly look at all that evidence and continue to hold him? I don't know if I've ever run across a greater miscarriage of justice."

"I've seen several greater injustices just this week," Frost said. "But that's why I do what I do."

"Since you're the expert, do you still think we can get him a retrial?"

"Maybe, but it's up to you and what other kind of facts you can get me."

Cal hung up, sighed, and looked at Kelly.

She stared knowingly at her husband.

"Looks like our trip to The Pirate's Den isn't going to be celebratory after all, is it?" she asked.

Cal shook his head. "Not in the least bit."

While they were walking toward the car, Cal's phone rang again, the screen displaying an unknown number.

"This is Cal," he said as he answered.

"Cal Murphy?" a man on the other end of the line asked.

"Yes. Who's this?"

"My name is Tripp Sloan, Susannah's brother. I heard you were workin' on a story about Isaiah Drake and my sister's murder. I'm on my way from Savannah to visit some friends in Pickett this weekend and would love to meet with you."

"How about dinner tonight at The Pirate's Den, say seven o'clock?" Cal asked.

"Perfect. See you then."

Cal hung up and looked at Kelly. "There's still hope for our visit to The Pirate's Den tonight. Tripp Sloan wants to talk."

CHAPTER 27

THE PIRATE'S DEN was crowded with customers celebrating the end of the work week. While waiting for a table,
Cal and Kelly endured a half hour of modern country pop,
songs about girls in blue jeans, boys with trucks, and people
everywhere drinking. The gray-bearded man nursing a bottle
of beer next to them launched into a tirade about the state
of country music.

"Country music sold its soul to the devil years ago," the
man said. "Nashville ain't put out a listenable song in fifteen
years."

"More 'an that," mumbled his drinking companion.

"Probably right. There ain't no Hank or young Waylon
Jennings or Merle Haggard to rescue us from this garbage."

"Don't we wish."

Cal and Kelly nodded in agreement, which was little
more than a polite gesture.

The gray-bearded man stared at Cal.

"Who's your favorite country music singer, buddy?" he
said, slapping Cal on the arm.

Cal squinted and looked skyward, all in an effort to give
him time to conjure up the name of at least one country mu-
sician from yesteryear. He was coming up empty.

"He loves the Charlie Daniels Band," Kelly said, saving him from sure scorn. "He loves the song about the devil going down to Georgia."

"Uh huh," the man said as he nodded. "Y'all ain't from 'round here, are ya?"

"What gave us away?" Cal asked with a slight grin.

"Y'all talk funny—both of ya."

The hostess called out, "Murphy, party of three. Murphy, party of three."

Cal exhaled, relieved to be saved from further critique about their mode of transportation or dress appearance compared to the majority of The Pirate's Den clientele. He and Kelly followed the young woman to their table.

"Where's the other member of your party?" she asked.

"He's on his way," Cal said. "Would you mind pointing him in our direction when he gets here?"

"Will do," she said, winking at Cal before she walked away.

"What do you think this is all about with Tripp Sloan?" Kelly asked.

"Maybe he wants to clear his conscience," Cal said. "Remember that Drake said he was hanging out with Tripp right here the night of Susannah's murder."

"Let's hope so."

When the waitress came around, Cal and Kelly both went for stronger drinks, ordering some craft beers from a Savannah brewery. They didn't have to wait long before Tripp Sloan slid into one of the empty chairs at their table.

"Tripp Sloan," he said, offering his hand to Cal and then Kelly. "It's so nice to meet y'all. My dad told me I should talk to you while I was here."

"Really?" Cal said. "And your father is Sheriff Sloan?"

Tripp nodded. "I see you've become fairly acquainted with him. He can be very off-putting at times."

"And threatening," Kelly said. "But let's not quibble over that."

Tripp nodded knowingly. "Well, I don't live in Pickett any more and never intend on returning. Draw your own conclusions about that, if you know what I mean."

Tripp flagged down the waitress, whose jaw dropped when he she recognized him. They talked for a minute before she scampered back to the kitchen to get his drink.

"Bekah and I went to Pickett County High together," Tripp said. "She was a freshman when I was a senior, but we stayed in touch until I moved away about eight years ago."

"So, why'd you move?" Cal asked.

"I think I've made it abundantly clear why I pulled up my roots and left," Tripp said. "I also had some job opportunities in Savannah that were far more lucrative than anything I'd ever get in Pickett."

"Okay, we don't want to hold you up here," Cal said as he leaned forward, "but let's cut to the chase. What can you tell us about the night of your sister's murder, Isaiah Drake, and anything else related to this case?"

Bekah handed Tripp a beer bottle, which he promptly began to peel the label off of. "Let me preface everything by saying I drank quite heavily that night," Tripp said. "And the next few nights after, to be honest. Losing Susannah was hard on my whole family. But to answer your question, that night wasn't all that unusual as I recall."

"You met Isaiah Drake here?" Cal asked.

Tripp nodded. "I wasn't the only one with Drake that night. My boy Jordan Hayward was here. Jacob Boone was here, though he was drinking with some other guys."

"When did Drake leave The Pirate's Den?"

Tripp pointed to a spot along the wall. "Drake was standing right there. He went to the bar to get a drink, stopped, and then made a dash for the parking lot."

"What did you do?"

"I followed him outside, of course, to see what was goin' on. He left so quickly. Then Jordan Hayward went after him. I was worried something was seriously wrong. Like maybe somebody had died or somethin'. Little did I know somebody was about to—and that would be my sister."

"Did you ask him why he was leaving?" Kelly asked.

"By the time I reached the parking lot, his Phantom was peelin' out onto the road."

"So, Hayward went with him?"

"I think so. I mean, eventually he showed back up at the bar by himself, but who really knows where he went. He said he didn't want to talk about it when he got back."

"What about Jacob Boone?" Cal asked.

"Oh, he left during that time and—"

"During what time?" Cal pressed.

"The time that Susannah was murdered, according to the coroner."

"And the police never questioned him?"

Tripp laughed. "You mean my dad? He was confident it was Drake and made sure that not only the charges stuck, but that he gave the prosecutor enough evidence to bury him."

Cal's eyes widened. "So, you think they got the wrong man?"

"I wouldn't doubt it. I think the evidence supports someone other than Drake. But that doesn't mean he didn't have anything to do with it." Tripp chuckled. "I tried to tell my dad that, but he wouldn't listen to me. Nailing Susannah's killer was Dad's top priority in life—but I think he only did that to make himself feel better. It certainly wasn't the justice-minded person who I knew him to be. It was like something snapped in my dad; I can't really explain it."

"So, who do you think did it?"

Tripp shrugged. "Maybe Drake or someone else. Could've been Jacob Boone."

CHAPTER 28

CAL CRANED HIS NECK and leaned forward to catch the numbers painted onto the mailboxes lined along the highway. He struggled to read each digit with nothing more than his car's high beams to illuminate them. Kelly called out addresses whenever one came into view for her.

"I think we're getting close," she said.

Cal adjusted his grip on the steering wheel.

"I just hope he's home."

After two intense minutes of searching for Jacob Boone's address that Tripp Sloan had given them over dinner, Cal and Kelly both expressed relief from the tedious exercise once the prescribed number appeared.

"Looks like he's home," Cal said, nodding toward the familiar pickup truck parked in the driveway.

Boone's home was a trailer situated on what Cal guessed to be an acre as he accounted for the neighbors on each side. In one of the back corners of the property, Cal noted a simple lean-to that provided cover for a couple of cars, neither of which looked road-worthy. They were both missing windshields and had at least one flat tire. An aging oak tree that supported an old tire swing was the lone vegetation in the front yard aside from knee-high weeds.

Cal rapped on the screen door, which was little more than a decoration based on the large number of holes and rips in it.

A few seconds later, Boone emerged wearing a bathrobe and holding a Bud Light.

"I thought I told you to leave me alone?" Boone said.

"I'm not very good at following directions," Cal quipped. "I trust that won't be a problem."

"Depends on why you're here. I've got little patience for rude people."

Cal eyed Boone closely before speaking.

"What exactly have we done to make you hate us so?" Cal asked.

"What haven't you done is more like it," Boone said before throwing back a long swig of beer.

"But you tried to run us off the road before we'd barely been here forty-eight hours."

"I already told you once, that wasn't me."

"Who else has access to your truck?" Kelly asked.

"Plenty of people. My friends know I leave my keys in the driver's side sun shade. Any one of them could've borrowed it that night."

"Who do you think borrowed it?"

"Jordan Hayward," Boone said. "He said something about needing to pick up a part from the salvage yard to get his car running for this weekend's annual Pickett County Demolition Derby out at the fairgrounds. The next thing I know, Hayward was gone, along with my truck."

"So, you're saying it wasn't you who ran us off the road?" Kelly asked.

"Look, lady, I put my days of overstepping the bounds of the law behind me a long time ago. And while I may not like you diggin' around my town and lookin' into my past, I'm certainly not gonna kill you just to get you to leave. I'm merely making a friendly suggestion."

"There's been little you've said or done that could be defined as friendly."

Boone huffed, fully stepped outside onto the small porch, and gazed up at the stars.

"Fine. I'll tell you whatever you wanna know as long as you promise to get outta here quick after I tell you to."

"Agreed," Cal said.

Boone drained the rest of his Bud Light before crushing the can against the porch rail. "What do you wanna know?"

"What do you remember about the night of May 7, 2004?"

"Aww, hell. I can barely remember what I ate for lunch, much less that far back."

Cal crossed his arms. "It's the night Susannah Sloan was murdered. Sound familiar now?"

"Why didn't you just say so? Of course I remember that night … well, most of it, anyway. I drank heavily for most of it."

"Was that at The Pirate's Den? Or somewhere else, perhaps?"

Boone took a deep breath. "Naw, it was *all* at The Pirate's Den."

"But you did leave at one point and come back?"

"Yeah, I left to go track down my boy Jordan Hayward."

"And why did he need to be tracked down?"

"Drake left The Pirate's Den in a huff, and Hayward went after him. But neither one of them were in any condition to drive."

"Yet you were?" Kelly asked.

"Back in the day, I could get away with anything and did. I practiced driving drunk so many times that I had it down to an art. I never got caught, though even if I did, I had a connection at the sheriff's department that could help me escape pretty much anything."

"But you didn't escape everything, did you?"

Boone bristled. "What's that supposed to mean?"

"Susannah Sloan effectively broke up your family and ripped your kids away from you, didn't she?"

"Well, yeah, but it was probably the best thing for me. It helped me get my life back on track and exit the world of crime. And I'd tell her as much if she were alive today."

"And just where exactly did you go when you left The Pirate's Den?"

Boone put his hands up, lifting them about chest high.

"I know how this is gonna sound, but I went to Susannah's house. I figured if Hayward was chasin' Drake, they'd both be at Susannah's house. And I was right."

"What happened when you got there?" Cal asked.

"Hayward was drunk and actin' crazy, crazier than usual. So, I grabbed him by the scruff of his neck and dragged him back to the car with me."

"And you just left Drake there?"

"I figured Drake was a big enough boy to get his own ride home," Boone said. "Besides, he didn't look like he was through talkin' to Susannah. She was cryin' and apologizin' for what she'd done, though she didn't act like she regretted it, just a woman sorry that she *had* to break up with him. I don't know. It was a long time ago, and my memory is a little foggy about all the details."

Cal pulled out his pad and jotted down a few notes. After a brief moment of silence, he refocused his attention on Hayward. "Anything else you feel might be very important?"

"Look, I told Sheriff Sloan all this when it happened. I never tried to hide anything from anybody, except maybe some reporters who came nosin' around Pickett, present company included. And while I still may have some issues with my anger, I don't hurt people any more. I've grown up."

"What about Hayward?"

Even with only a dim yellow porch light to illuminate Boone's face, Cal observed the man tense up.

"Why were you out at Bee Gum Lake before anyone else? We saw you there," Cal said.

Boone bit his lip and narrowed his eyes. "I was just tryin' to help Hayward out. He was in a tight spot and asked me for a favor, so I agreed. We were supposed to meet farther south along the highway, but he never made it."

"What were you meeting all the way out there for?"

"All I know is that he asked me to help him out. That's all. I don't know exactly what he wanted, but whatever it was, he wanted to keep it a secret. And it was obviously for a good reason, though he wasn't secretive enough apparently. I waited and waited before I decided to call it a day and drive back to Pickett. That's when I saw all the cop cars out there and decided to see what was goin' on."

"So, who had reason to kill Hayward?"

"Plenty of people, I suppose. He ran with a rough crowd."

"What about Sheriff Sloan?"

Boone shrugged. "I don't know. But the one thing I know after growin' up and livin' in this town as long as I have is people aren't always what they seem, present company included."

Kelly forced a smile. "If I didn't know any better, Mr. Boone, I'd think you were changing your tune about us."

"People can change their minds if they want to. It's a free country."

"Thanks for your help," Cal said. "I want to be fair to all the parties involved when I write my story."

"You're welcome. But be careful. There are still plenty of people around here who don't like their private lives or their pasts peeled open like a can of sardines. I suggest you get outta here before somethin' happens to you."

"Everybody keeps saying that," Cal said. "Is there someone in Pickett who's actually planning on hurting us?"

"Not that I know of," Boone said. "But like I said, people aren't always what they seem in Pickett."

Once Cal and Kelly retreated to the privacy of their car, Kelly sighed and turned to Cal.

"You believe anything that guy said?" she asked.

Cal shrugged. "He spun a good yarn, but I'm not buying anything anybody in this town says. But I'll take Jacob Boone's own advice and remember that *people aren't always what they seem in Pickett.*"

CHAPTER 29

CAL COULDN'T SLEEP WELL that night and around 6:00 a.m. finally decided against trying any more. He got dressed and went downstairs at the Okefenokee Inn to get some coffee and pore over his notes. If there was anything that was clear at this point it was that Drake deserved a new trial, if for nothing else than his poor defense team and a shoddy investigation by the Pickett County Sheriff's Department. But a new suspect seemed elusive.

Over the next two hours, Cal concocted several theories about who could've murdered Susannah and why. He even created a theory for Drake—and Boone, too. After all, Boone told Cal twice the night before that people aren't always what they seem.

Present company included.

Cal chuckled to himself. Boone didn't appear to be a likely suspect, but Cal wasn't going to rule him out simply because he showed a human side with empathy while chatting on the porch. But there was one piece of information that emerged from the conversation with Boone that bugged Cal.

Boone told Sheriff Sloan about the convergence of three men—Boone, Hayward, and Drake—at Susannah's house that night. But Cal didn't remember reading about that in any of the trial transcripts. Surely, even a half-witted lawyer would've questioned Boone at trial. But Boone never took the stand.

Cal dialed Robert Sullivan, Drake's lawyer, to question him about it.

"Mr. Murphy, it's quite early on a Saturday morning for you to be calling me. Good thing I'm still in Georgia and not back in Seattle."

"You're still here?" Cal asked, somewhat surprised.

"Yeah, just getting in a round of golf this morning. Tee time is in five minutes, so make this quick."

"Last night, I spoke to a guy who claimed to be at Susannah Sloan's house the night of her murder—a guy by the name of Jacob Boone. Does that ring any bells for you?"

"Nope. Never heard of him."

"Well, that's odd," Cal said. "He told me this last night and said Sheriff Sloan questioned him during the investigation."

"It wasn't in the discovery."

"Are you sure?"

"If I could, I'd let you dig through my trial notes. But I swear to you I've never heard of the man, that name, or any other claims that someone else was at Susannah's house the night she was murdered other than Drake."

In the background, Cal heard what sounded like a familiar voice calling for Sullivan.

"Sorry, but I gotta run. We can talk about this on Monday if you've got more questions."

Cal hung up and shook his head. He drew several conclusions about Sheriff Sloan: Sloan was either inept or hiding something—or both. Cal's curiosity was also piqued about the familiar voice he heard in the background of his call with Sullivan.

Could that be who I think it is?

Cal started pounding away on his computer, using search engines to establish a connection between Sullivan and the voice of the other man.

After a couple of simple searches, Cal's jaw dropped.

Would you look at that?

Robert Sullivan graduated at the top of his law class at Emory University. The student who graduated second in his class at Emory that same year? None other than Hal Golden.

***

ARMED WITH KNOWLEDGE of this suspicious connection, Cal contacted Larry Arant at *The Searchlight* to see if he'd be willing to meet and compare notes about the case with him and Kelly. Surprisingly, Arant agreed.

Arant had a large pot of coffee brewing when Cal and Kelly stepped into the nearly deserted office.

"Big day today down at the track," Arant said. "If you're going to chase anyone down to speak with them about this case, that's where you'll need to do it."

"Except you," Kelly said with a smile.

"The track isn't my thing, but we will have a photographer there—well, our only photographer will be there. I'll hear about it from everyone else without having to suffer through the deafening roar of those suped-up cars."

Satisfied with the amount of coffee in the pot, Arant pulled it off and poured the black liquid into their mugs.

"But we didn't come here to talk about the derby, did we?" Arant asked as he handed Cal and Kelly their cups.

"No, we came here to talk about this Drake case with you one last time," Cal said.

"Just once more? *Promise?*" Arant quipped.

"I'm doing my job," Cal said. "If you're not thorough, you'll get burned."

"Or sued," Kelly added.

"Oh, I know about all that far too well," Arant said.

"Okay, so what I don't get is how no one else was brought up as a suspect," Cal said. "I haven't seen it in any of the articles I read about the trial, but did Sullivan ever try to make the case that someone else could've murdered Susannah other than Drake?"

Arant stirred his coffee, adding in cream and sugar. "He made vague references to it, but that was the problem with his defense. It was always some other nameless and faceless man who did this to Susannah. Never once did he raise the possibility that it was someone in the community or even outside of it who killed her. In a nutshell, the defense he used was *my client didn't do it. He's innocent. He loved her. He couldn't have done this.* Predictably, it failed."

"So, the investigation never veered away from Drake?" Cal asked.

"Never. It was Drake from the first day until the last. It was backward if you ask me. Sheriff Sloan determined it was Drake and did everything in his power to make sure he gathered the evidence necessary for conviction."

"It worked," Cal said, "but I'm not sure he got the right man."

"At the time of the trial, a few people thought somebody else killed Susannah, but the majority believed Drake did it. You'll always find some people around here who think it was a conspiracy and some kind of cover up. However, all that talk was in generalities, nothing specific."

"Who did people suspect the most?"

"Jacob Boone comes to mind," Arant said with a shrug. "When Boone realized he was losing his kids forever, it was one of the most painful moments I've ever witnessed in a courtroom. He'd definitely have motive."

"Anyone else?"

"Some people brought up Jordan Hayward, which very well could've been the case, but we'll never know it now."

"Is that all?"

"Oh, no. Sheriff Sloan's name got floated around. However, he's enjoyed such a favored status in the city, I find it hard to believe you'd get a true objective sense of him from the community."

"That's quite a list to add to Drake's name," Cal said. "Those are the four I came up with as I've been researching this story."

Arant nodded knowingly. "And while those are four good suspects, they aren't the only ones."

"There's a fifth person?" Cal asked incredulously.

"Don't laugh too hard, but Devontae Ray is another name that got tossed around."

"*Devonate Ray?* The guy confined to a wheelchair? What motive would he have?"

Arant scratched the back of his head and looked at his coffee. "You'd be surprised. He's actually got more reason than anyone to kill her."

"Really?"

"I'm shootin' ya straight. Ray's been through a lot, most of it at the hands in some way or another with the Sloan family."

"Please explain," Cal said, pulling out his notebook.

"You've been here a week, and this story hasn't come up?" Arant asked. "Hard to believe."

"Not a peep."

"Well, there are two things that happened. The first is that Ray's older brother, Phillip, was arrested on a felony burglary charge … along with Drake. Phillip was eighteen, and Sloan charged him, resulting in a conviction. However, Drake was only questioned and released. People here said it was because Drake was committed to Auburn and Sloan's a big fan of the school's football team. Who knows why? But it was devastating for Phillip, who had scholarship offers from Florida State and many other schools around the south to play football. After the conviction, all of Phillip's offers were rescinded."

"And the second thing that happened?"

"This was the big one: Susannah was the driver who hit Devontae while he was riding tandem with Phillip. Phillip died in the accident, while Devontae became paralyzed in his legs. It was a sad day around Pickett. Susannah was home visiting from college and had been at The Pirate's Den, drinking with some friends. She claimed she wasn't drunk, and her blood alcohol level came back at zero. And then it was simply ruled an accident. Devontae has only grown more and more bitter through the years. But at the time, he was bitter and visibly angry. Whenever anyone saw him out in the community, Devontae wore a scowl on his face."

"But he's confined to a wheelchair and paralyzed, correct?" Cal asked.

Arant nodded. "That's why it's ludicrous to some degree. If Ray did it, he'd have to have some help—not to mention getting someone to actually pull the trigger for him. There's no way he could've gotten into her house on his own."

"Let's not waste our time on him," Cal said. "We need to focus on the viable suspects in this case."

"Those are all the names I heard at the time and through the years. The honest truth is I have no idea now who did it. Every one of them could be guilty, if you ask me."

CHAPTER 30

CAL GAWKED AT THE CROWD filing into the Pickett County Fairgrounds just before 11:00 a.m. Living in the south, he had seen his share of southern culture that would bewilder anyone unfamiliar with its customs and rituals. But the people attending the annual Walk the Plank Demolition Derby seemed like a hidden culture that had just been discovered and documented in a *National Geographic* special. The south didn't hold a monopoly on demolition derbies—or banger racing, as they were called in England—but it did on the people who enjoyed the sport.

He looked over at Kelly, whose eyes managed to widen even more than his own.

"What do you think of this?" he asked.

Speechless, she simply shook her head.

Pickup trucks elevated by a hydraulic system bounced up and down to the beat of a hard-driving country music song. Gun racks decorated the back windows of more trucks than even the sticker of Calvin from Calvin and Hobbes fame taking a leak on the owner's most-hated NASCAR driver. One elderly woman glared at Cal when he didn't stop fast enough for her at a cross walk. She proceeded to salute him with her middle finger, pull her sweater back to reveal her handgun, and spew a stream of tobacco onto the hood of his rental car.

"Do you think she's really a woman?" Kelly finally asked.

Cal nodded. "Most of the women I've met in my travels to the rural south are as sweet as a glass of iced tea. But there are always a few who seem to defy the status quo. She'd fall into the latter category."

They followed the parking attendants' directions, parking next to a 1940s era pickup truck on the right. Seconds later, a beat-up Suburban from the 1980s pulled up next to them on the left. Over the track's loudspeaker, an announcer gave a rundown of the day's events, starting with several short races before the flag dropped to start the derby.

Cal bought a pair of tickets and entered the turnstile with Kelly. Before they arrived at their seats, everyone stopped and faced the flag, first for Lee Greenwood's rendition of *God Bless the USA*, followed by Miss Pickett County singing *The National Anthem*. The anthem performance sounded somewhat familiar despite a few dropped words and changes to the lyrics where bombs burst in air not once but twice.

"I hope singing isn't what she does for the talent portion of those pageants," Kelly whispered.

Cal chuckled and took a seat. Kelly, meanwhile, headed back down the aisle and slipped into the stream of the late-arriving crowd. She'd told Cal she wanted to take some pictures for her portfolio, surmising that this would be her only opportunity to photograph such a unique event.

Using his binoculars, Cal watched the pits to see if there was anything interesting happening. He also wanted to watch any of the people he viewed as suspects in the case and hopefully interview them one last time before heading home.

He felt as if he was more confounded about the death of Susannah Sloan than he was before he left Seattle. He still had no idea who killed her—and he still hadn't ruled out Isaiah Drake either.

Jacob Boone revved up his car before climbing out and grinning maniacally at several of the other drivers. Sheriff Sloan walked around the corner of a white cinder block building on the infield where it appeared a driver's meeting was set to occur. He motioned to Boone to join him.

I wonder what that's all about.

Cal put his binoculars down to glance at the order of events. When he looked back up, he saw Boone disappear around the corner where Sloan had been. Cal strained his neck to catch any further action but was derailed when Crazy Corey Taylor stepped into his line of sight toting a sign proclaiming, "The End is Near!"

Exasperated, Cal put his binoculars away and sighed, gesturing for Taylor to move along. Taylor obliged, dancing and spinning as he moved down the aisle. He also repeated the message on his sign, yelling it. Taylor's antics led to at least three children breaking into tears.

Cal returned to watching the pits when Taylor returned, this time interrupting Cal by leaning over and whispering in his ear. "Figure out who did it yet?" Taylor asked. "If you want to know who did it, come find me sometime."

* * *

THE SOUND OF METAL colliding with metal at fifteen to twenty-five miles per hour echoed across the grandstand, always followed by a chorus of oohs and ahhs. Cal understood the appeal of watching cars ram one another for sport. The singular objective to destroy the other competitors and be the remaining operational car took away the pretense that a race was necessary. It was a vehicular gladiator event. And even as someone who was uninitiated, Cal enjoyed it.

Jacob Boone was one of the final two competitors but lost when Earl Underwood clipped the back of his car, which proceeded to flip and land wheels up. Boone climbed out and signaled that he was okay, leading to Earl's attempt at a victory donut. However, Earl couldn't generate enough speed, and he instead settled on a celebratory flip after climbing out of his car.

While the crowd cheered Earl's win, Cal was walking down the steps to meet Kelly when he noticed a pair of reporters with cameramen interviewing Sheriff Sloan. Cal hustled over to see what they were questioning him about.

"We understand that the FBI has taken over the investigation of Jordan Hayward's death," one of the reporters said. "Can you tell us anything you learned before ceding jurisdiction?"

Sloan grimaced. "I'm not really authorized to comment on the crime scene at this time, but I will say it was unusual."

"So is it safe to assume that this wasn't a suicide?" the reporter asked.

"No, this wasn't a suicide," Sloan confirmed.

"Could this be the work of the Marsh Monster?" the other reporter asked, tongue-in-cheek.

Sloan's eyes narrowed. "A man's dead and you want to make a joke like that? The Marsh Monster may not be a monster in the way we think of them, but whoever he is, he's killed a couple of good people in Pickett. And it's no laughing matter."

The reporter turned beet red and slunk back.

Cal stepped forward to ask a question, but Sloan noticed him.

"That's all I've got time for," Sloan said before he turned and hopped over a barrier wall, distancing himself from the media members.

Cal watched Sloan until he vanished from sight. Cal was still staring when he felt a tug on his sleeve.

"Cal! Cal! Hello? Earth to Cal?"

Cal blinked and realized Kelly was standing right there. "Oh, hey. Did you get some good photos?"

She grinned. "Did I ever? However, there's one you'll be particularly interested in. Here."

She handed Cal her camera.

He looked at the small display screen.

"Zoom in," she said.

Cal followed her instructions and enlarged an image of Sheriff Sloan and Jacob Boone exchanging a large duffle bag.

"Go to the next picture," Kelly said.

Cal scrolled to the next photo and zoomed in to see Boone staring into the opened bag which appeared to contain several stacks of cash.

"Jacob Boone was right," Kelly said. "People aren't always what they seem in Pickett."

CHAPTER 31

CAL AND KELLY MANAGED to beat the rush to Curly's Diner, which quickly became packed with race attendees. They nodded to Curly, who brought them a menu and two glasses of sweet tea.

"If you two stay here another few days, you'll be able to order *the usual*, and I'll know what you mean," Curly said with a smile.

"No offense, but we'd like to avoid that," Cal said.

"I understand. I wouldn't want to stay around a place where I was making so many enemies."

"Are people talking about us?" Kelly asked.

Curly broke into a wry grin. "This is Pickett. Everybody talks about everybody." He tapped on the table. "I'll give you two a minute to decide and be back."

Cal waited until Curly disappeared into the kitchen before he started talking. "I feel like we're in a demolition derby ourselves here trying to figure this case out," Cal said. "We don't have enough definitive proof to get Drake exonerated yet—if he even deserves to be exonerated—and we've watched our list of suspects reduced to one … but only because he's dead."

"Hayward's death doesn't get him off the hook," Kelly said.

Cal nodded. "True, but it does make helping Drake clear his name that much more difficult."

"So, let's go through all our suspects," Kelly said. "Start with Sheriff Sloan. Motive?"

"Racism? Disgust? Protecting his family's honor?"

"I could possibly see the first one, but protecting his family's honor? It's the 21st Century. Who doesn't have a daughter these days bringing shame upon her family name? The Kardashians even *celebrate* their shame."

Cal huffed. "Let's stay focused. We could lament the downfall of our entire country once we start talking about reality show *celebrities*, particularly ones known for their abnormally large body parts."

"Good point."

Curly returned and took their orders before moving to the next table.

"So let's say Sloan *is* a racist and didn't want his daughter marrying a black man. Why not kill Drake instead?" Cal asked.

"Less blowback. Easier to get away with killing your daughter than killing a superstar athlete."

"Or easier to hire someone to kill your daughter," Cal countered.

"You think he hired someone like Jacob Boone?"

"Possibly. I wouldn't rule that out. But all we know for sure is that Sloan has something to hide."

"And he'll keep on hiding it, too. With his ability to doctor the logs, no one is going to believe what we found out about Sloan being logged out during the time of Susannah's death. We're just going to seem like a pair of sad muckrakers."

Cal laughed. "We've been called worse."

"What about Jordan Hayward? His motive?"

"Jealousy. He didn't want anyone taking his girl away, even his best friend."

Kelly furrowed her brow. "So, he murders her?"

"Could've been a crime of passion, and then he thought he'd be able to pin it on Drake."

"But Drake can't remember anything. How'd he pull that off?"

"Maybe Drake didn't see it. What if Hayward knocked Drake out and then killed Susannah before Hayward decided to frame one of his best friends?"

Kelly nodded. "Hayward was the beneficiary to Drake's fortune ... whatever is left of it at this point."

"It'd be worth finding out who's the beneficiary of Drake's money now that Hayward's gone. Might at least give us motive for Hayward's death."

"Of course, Hayward's motivation would be the same as Drake's, albeit jealousy over a different guy."

Curly slipped Cal and Kelly's meals onto the table.

"Enjoy," Curly said before he scurried away. Cal and Kelly began to attack their meals.

"And Boone?" Kelly asked after getting down her first bite.

"He's got revenge as a motive. Susannah Sloan effectively took his kids away from him. I don't care how he tries to portray himself now, that's a pain that doesn't just go away."

"Should I even bring up Devontae Ray?"

Cal shook his head. "That just seems like a reach, though I wouldn't rule it out at this point. Maybe he was working with Boone."

"But do we have any indication that those two run in the same circles?"

Cal shrugged. "Not yet, but it's worth considering, even if it seems farfetched."

Cal's phone buzzed on the table.

"Who is it?" Kelly asked.

"Marsha Frost from The Innocence Alliance. This should be interesting." Cal answered his phone. "This is Cal."

"Hi, Cal. This is Marsha. I've got some big news."

"Oh? Go on."

"A federal judge stepped in on behalf of Isaiah Drake and ordered a new trial. But not only that, the judge ordered Drake to be released immediately."

Cal smiled and mouthed the news to Kelly. "So, where's Drake now?"

"Not sure," Frost said. "Robert Sullivan wasn't readily available to help him get released, but apparently Drake talked one of the prison guards into releasing him by giving the guy an autographed football for his son."

"Any idea where he's headed?" Cal asked.

"If I had to guess, I'd say he was headed straight for Pickett."

"We'll be on the look out for him," Cal said.

"Be careful, Cal. When I spoke to Drake, he was acting a little strange."

"Strange? How?"

"Like he's angry and mad. And he wants revenge."

"Revenge on who?"

Frost sighed. "He's convinced Sheriff Sloan was the one who killed Susannah. And he's also convinced she'll never get justice."

"That doesn't sound like a good situation."

"I know. Just be careful and watch out for him," Frost said. "I would hate for him to become the person everyone believed he was years ago."

CHAPTER 32

UNDAUNTED BY SHERIFF SLOAN'S WARNINGS, Cal and Kelly decided to make yet another run at him. Armed with a picture that demanded answers, Cal knew his journalistic reputation would be held suspect if he didn't at least give Sloan a chance to answer for the suspicious nature of the photo.

After freshening up at the Okefenokee Inn, Cal and Kelly headed to Sloan's house. With a dirt driveway that stretched more than 200 meters, Sloan had the modern day equivalent of a moat. It was clear he didn't want to be bothered, yet if someone dared to attempt contact, he'd see the person coming and could prepare in plenty of time.

The moment Cal pulled into Sloan's long drive and began rattling along with driveway, Sloan looked up and glared at him. Sloan was outside with a trailer hitched to his truck. One of the unidentifiable cars from the demolition derby sat on the trailer as Sloan appeared to be hammering on the body of the vehicle before he stopped and walked toward the driveway to meet his uninvited guest.

Cal came to a stop twenty yards from Sloan's house, a sprawling brick ranch decorated by a handful of ungroomed bushes beneath each window and an antique weather vane perched atop the roof. But Cal didn't stop on his own volition: Sloan, wielding a sledge hammer, stood in the middle of the driveway.

"You ready for this?" Cal asked Kelly.

She nodded. "Are you?"

Cal shrugged. "I guess we'll find out."

They both exited the vehicle and approached Sloan, who remained stoic.

"How many times does a man need to tell a couple of reporters that they aren't welcome any more?" Sloan bellowed.

Cal forced a smile. "My teachers always told me I didn't have the best listening comprehension skills."

"They were right," Sloan deadpanned.

"Look, I know we've been a thorn in your side this week, but it's for a good reason: We don't want to see an innocent man die."

Sloan shook his head. "If you keep comin' around here when you've been warned, people won't see you as so innocent."

Cal sighed. "I'm going to take that as a joke and not a threat."

"You shouldn't take it that way," Sloan said, throwing the sledge hammer over his shoulder.

"Sheriff Sloan, we have a few more questions for you," Kelly said before pausing and taking a deep breath, "like this picture of you handing over a duffle bag full of cash to Jacob Boone."

"I swear to God, if this was the wild west, I would've dropped you two a long time ago," Sloan said with a sneer.

"But it's not, is it?" Cal shot back. "And it's difficult to get away with murder twice, I hear."

Sloan's knuckles whitened around the handle of the hammer as he stepped forward.

"Just what exactly are you insinuating, Mr. Murphy?" Sloan asked.

"I think it's pretty clear," Cal said. "At least, it certainly will appear that way in my story if you refuse to answer a few simple questions. I mean, I can't help what the public takeaway will be from the article when I write that you declined to comment. If an FBI probe begins surrounding the practices of your sheriff's department as a result, you can't blame me for that either."

Sloan took a deep breath but remained silent for almost a minute. When he finally spoke, he lost his edge, apparently resigned to the fact that Cal had painted him into a corner.

"What do you wanna know?" Sloan asked.

Before Cal could answer, the roar of a car storming down Sloan's driveway arrested the attention of everyone. Cal spun around to see a vehicle kicking up a cloud of dust as it hurtled toward Sloan's house.

"You know who that is?" Cal asked.

Sloan didn't move. "Got no idea, but whoever they are, they're going to have a lot to answer for after tearing up my driveway like that."

The car skidded to a stop just behind Cal and Kelly's vehicle. When the dust settled, Cal identified the car as a white Ford Mustang but still couldn't make out who the driver was. When the door swung open, Cal noticed the gun in the man's hand before he recognized the man's face.

Isaiah Drake.

Sloan didn't appear intimidated by Drake's gun, walking toward the uninvited guest as opposed to cowering away from him.

"What the hell are you doin' here?" Sloan demanded.

Cal stepped to the side, unsure if he should get involved or not.

Drake kept his gun trained on Sloan. "I'll answer your questions after you answer mine, starting with why did you kill her, Sheriff Sloan? Why did you kill your only daughter? Why did you *murder* Susannah?"

Sloan glared at Drake. "How dare you come on to my property and accuse me of such a thing. It wasn't you who had to bury his own daughter. I'm givin' you ten seconds to get back in your car and get outta here before I have you arrested and thrown right back where you came from."

"I'm not here to negotiate," Drake said. "I've dreamed of this moment for a long time—and there's only one of us who'll be leaving your property alive tonight … and I'm the one holding a weapon."

Sloan slipped his right hand into his pocket.

"No, no, no," Drake said. "Keep your hands where I can see them."

Sloan pulled his right hand out of his pocket and returned it to the handle of his sledge hammer. "Well, nobody ever accused you of bein' smart," Sloan said. "If it wasn't for me convincin' Mrs. Danford to change your History grade, you would've ended up at some junior college in a Kansas prairie somewhere instead of playin' college football at a top-tier program."

"Susannah deserved better."

Sloan laughed nervously. "She sure did. And she was tryin' to get it with a respectable lawyer from Jacksonville before you took that—and her very life—away from her just like *that*," Sloan said, snapping for emphasis.

"You were always the best at coming up with a way to

avoid responsibility … or maybe you forgot that one of your deputies ended up in prison. He told me the whole story about your wife's death. Suicide, my ass."

"You watch yourself, Isaiah," Sloan said, wagging a finger at him.

Drake glanced at Cal before turning his attention back toward Sloan.

"What? You don't want this reporter here to know the truth, though I'm not even sure I believe the version your deputy told me."

"Don't even think about goin' there, Isaiah. I swear to God—"

"You swear you'll do to me what you did to her?" Drake asked. "It was an *accident*, right? Your gun discharged while you were cleaning it. You weren't being careful. You killed your wife. Or maybe you did it on purpose. She committed suicide? And poor Susannah went to her grave at your hands, believing her mother couldn't handle this life anymore."

"You watch it, Isaiah. I swear—"

"Stop swearing and make me stop, if you're man enough. I know what you did that night. I know you killed her."

Cal recognized the situation was near a boiling point. In a matter of seconds, Drake was going to pull the trigger and kill Sloan. And then Cal had no idea what would happen after that, but he was sure it wouldn't be a desirable outcome for anyone involved. He scanned the area for Kelly, who had moved to the side when Drake first exited his vehicle and was capturing the entire incident on her camera.

"Let's not do anything we'll regret, okay," Cal said, placing both of his hands in the air.

"I'll regret *not* doing this," Drake said.

"I didn't kill Susannah," Sloan said. "It wasn't me."

Drake's hand shook as he started to walk slowly toward Sloan. "Enough of your lies. I heard them in my head every day for almost twelve years."

A tear streaked down Sloan's face. "I miss her too. Not a day goes by that I don't think about her, about how she could've had a different life, a happy life."

"Put the gun down," Cal said to Drake. "It's not worth it. Killing Sheriff Sloan won't bring back Susannah."

Drake's gaze darted back and forth between Cal and Sloan. "No, it won't. But it will get justice for her."

"What type of justice will you be gettin' if you murder an innocent man?" Sloan asked.

"You're not innocent," Drake roared before cocking his gun.

Cal then took a drastic measure, stepping directly in front of Drake. "He may not be innocent, but I am," Cal said. "Put the gun down."

In the distance, sirens wailed.

Cal looked past Drake to see a pair of deputy cars flying down Sloan's driveway.

"It's over," Cal said. "Any justice you think you'll be ex-acting will be negated by the narrative my peers will write about you. Do the right thing and throw your gun to the side before it gets worse for you."

Drake dropped his gun and staggered to the ground. Tears began to roll down his face.

"But I miss her *so* much," Drake said. "I can't help but think about Susannah every single day."

"Me, too, Isaiah," Sloan said, kneeling down next to Drake. "I miss her, too."

The deputy cars came to a halt behind Drake's Mustang. The doors opened and then slammed as a pair of deputies rushed toward the scene.

Sloan held up his hand, gesturing toward the deputies to stand down. He proceeded to put his arm around Drake in a comforting move. "And if you missed her so much, maybe you shouldn't have killed her," Sloan said, before kicking Drake in the ribs. "Arrest him."

Sloan stepped back as his deputies rushed in and wrestled a resistant Drake to the ground before handcuffing him.

Cal watched in somewhat disbelief over the scene that unfolded. He wasn't sure which was more unfathomable—Drake threatening Sheriff Sloan with a gun or Sloan feigning empathy before kicking Drake and having him arrested. Deputy Tillman helped Drake to his feet before glancing at Cal, who read the look of a deputy feeling conflicted.

Sloan sauntered over to Cal. The sheriff slipped a toothpick in his mouth and crossed his arms.

"Any doubt that man's not stable?" Sloan asked. "He threatened me with a gun for God's sake. It was nice theater, but he's guilty, and I can't wait to watch him get another guilty verdict." He worked his toothpick over and waited a moment before continuing. "I don't think I need to answer another single question of yours."

Cal cocked his head to one side and eyed the sheriff closely. "Actually, you do," Cal said as he held up his iPad for Sloan to view. "Care to explain this to me?"

Sloan inspected the photo of himself handing Boone a bag of cash. "No, I don't," Sloan roared. "Now get off my property and outta my town before I make your life a livin' hell."

Cal glanced at Kelly, who was already walking back toward their car. He joined her, satisfied that she had captured a telling moment in the investigation; yet it was a moment that was no closer to leading them to the truth about what happened to Susannah Sloan.

CHAPTER 33

AFTER SPENDING THE REMAINDER of Saturday working on an article about Isaiah Drake's release and subsequent arrest for *The Seattle Times*, Cal and Kelly decided to attend Pickett AME Church on Sunday morning. Cal thought it would help give him more depth to the feature story he was writing on Drake.

They slipped into the church five minutes after the service began, snagging the last two empty slots along the back pew. Bishop Jermaine Arnold started preaching after a lengthy session of singing hymns with the lively congregation. He paced back and forth across the stage for the first fifteen minutes before venturing down into the aisles. His sermon on the children of Israel escaping the Egyptians into the desert brought some moans and a smattering of "come on now" exclamations from the audience.

"There are times in our lives where we may feel like we're the ones being persecuted, like there are a different set of rules for us based on factors beyond our control," Bishop Arnold said. "Perhaps it has to do with the color of our skin or the hand we've been dealt in life. We might be poor and look at a rich person and think he has no problems. Or we might find ourselves fortunate to have money yet look at the poor person and wonder what it would be like to be so unencumbered by so much responsibility. No matter where God has placed us on this earth and what we look like and what kind of job we might or might not have, what's important for us as God's children is to remember that our joy is not found in how we might feel about our current situation; no, our joy is found in our obedience to the one we claim to follow."

Arnold continued down the aisle until he reached the back row. He stood right next to Cal and Kelly.

"This has been an interesting week in our community. We've lost someone we've known and loved and watched grow up here in Jordan Hayward. We've also found Isaiah Drake, who returned to us—even if ever so briefly—after being falsely accused of murder. We must all endeavor to show love to those around us this week and remember that no matter how difficult or trying our situation might be, it's not permanent. Nothing is forever … except God and his love for his people."

A rousing round of "Amens" erupted throughout the sanctuary. Bishop Arnold smiled as he returned to the stage. He said a prayer that lasted at least five minutes by Cal's count before the choir sang another song and Bishop Arnold dismissed the congregation.

Cal and Kelly exited the sanctuary but didn't leave the church grounds. Cal saw Hayward's mother, who he wanted to talk to, as well as several other people who looked like they might be willing to share their feelings about all the events that had happened over the past week.

Cal interviewed a couple of churchgoers briefly before he saw Heloise Hayward, Jordan's mother. He walked up to her and looked her in the eyes.

"Sorry for your loss, Mrs. Hayward. I know your Jordan meant a lot to you," Cal said.

Mrs. Hayward closed her eyes and nodded slowly.

Cal continued. "Look, I know our last conversation wasn't exactly the best one and—"

"No need to apologize," Mrs. Hayward said, interrupting. "I know we all get carried away sometimes in our judgments and presuppositions. Jordan wasn't all I hoped he would be, but he tried. Sometimes he tried hard; sometimes he didn't. But he always wanted to do the right thing even when it didn't look that way, that much I sincerely believe."

Kelly hugged Mrs. Hayward and patted her on the back. "Be strong, Mrs. Hayward."

Mrs. Hayward forced a smile. "That's the state of my life, child."

Cal and Kelly stepped back, giving way to a short line of well-wishers wanting to speak with Mrs. Hayward. They watched as several women gave her a hug. Devontae Ray then wheeled up next to her. She leaned down to hug him. Ray was followed by Harold Jenkins, one of Drake's former teammates from the Pickett County High School football team. Cal waited until Jenkins was clearly finished with Mrs. Hayward before approaching him.

"Harold Jenkins?" Cal said.

Jenkins nodded. "And you are?"

"Cal Murphy, *The Seattle Times*," Cal said, offering his hand.

Jenkins narrowed his eyes before he leaned back, withdrawing in a way that demonstrated he held Cal suspect.

"What do you want?" Jenkins asked.

"I was wondering if you might be interested in talking a little bit about Isaiah Drake?"

"What for?"

"I'm writing an article on Drake for my paper, and I thought you might be able to provide a little bit more depth as to who he was—and maybe still is."

Jenkins furrowed his brow. "Why would I want to do that?"

"No reason other than maybe you're interested in helping let others know the truth about who Drake really is and what kind of man he was when you knew him."

Jenkins chuckled. "We weren't men when I knew him. We were just kids … crazy stupid kids."

"Even the night that he supposedly killed Susannah Sloan?"

Jenkins scowled. "I'm not sure what you're trying to get at, Mr. …"

"Murphy. Cal Murphy."

"Mr. Murphy. All I know I know is that Isaiah Drake didn't kill the sheriff's daughter that night. No way. He loved that girl too much."

"Enough that he might not want anyone else to have her if he couldn't?" Cal asked.

Jenkins shook his head. "Not a chance. He actually cherished her. He even confessed to me the day before she died that he'd never slept with her. Can you believe that? A man in this day and age with a woman who looks that good and they never slept together? Unreal."

"And you believed him?"

Jenkins sighed. "What kind of idiot brags about that these days? Of course I believed him. Drake was a gentleman through and through."

"So, who else could've done this?" Cal asked. "Who else had the motive and desire? What is this town collectively hiding?"

"Nobody's hidin' nothin'," Jenkins said. "Not even Sheriff Sloan."

"Wait. What do you mean by that?" Cal asked.

"How long you been here, Mr. Murphy? A week?"

"Sounds about right."

"You've been here a week, and nobody has brought up how corrupt the sheriff is?"

Cal shook his head. "That's not where I focused my concern."

"Well, you should have because Sheriff Sloan is about as crooked as they come. He's so corrupt that he doesn't even try to cover it up any more."

"Cover what up?" Cal asked.

"His moonshine ring, led by none other than Jacob Boone."

Cal's eyed Jenkins suspiciously. "Sheriff Sloan? Running moonshine?"

Jenkins waved his hands. "No, no. Not like that. He just ensures that Jacob Boone doesn't have any problems running it. He protects him. You know—you scratch my back, I'll scratch yours."

Cal shot a glance at Kelly, who'd remained silent throughout the exchange.

"And everybody knows about this?" he asked.

Jenkins shrugged. "It's pretty common knowledge. At least, that's what I hear."

"How long has this been going on?" Cal asked.

"I first heard about it around the time Susannah Sloan was murdered."

"Before or after?" Cal asked.

"Before. Maybe a month or two before. It was all the gossip in Pickett."

"Why?"

"Because if the sheriff was doing something illegal, who was going to prosecute him? His daughter? Nah, I don't think so. It seemed fishy from the first time I heard it."

"And this moonshine ring is generally regarded as fact?"

"Of course. It's Pickett, man. Anything goes here. In fact, you can just about get away with anything here if you know the right people."

"Meaning Sheriff Sloan?"

Jenkins glanced around before he nodded.

"One more question for you, if that's all right," Cal said.

"Go ahead."

"I heard you were with Drake at The Pirate's Den the night of Susannah Sloan's murder. Is that right?"

Jenkins nodded.

"What do you remember about that night then?"

Jenkins sighed and looked skyward, shaking his head.

"I try not to think about it, but I have a pretty clear memory. I wasn't drinking like everybody else. I was supposed to be the designated driver, if anybody needed one."

"Did they?" Cal asked.

"Pretty much everybody did, but I wasn't very good at it."

"Why do you say that?"

"Because several of the guys left in the middle of our time there before I could stop them."

"What happened?"

"Well, Drake, Hayward, Tripp Sloan, and myself were all having a good time. I remember seeing Jacob Boone there with his crew, too. It was fun, reliving our glory days playing for Pickett County. But something happened that set Drake off. He rushed toward the door. Hayward followed him."

"Did you follow them?"

"Not immediately," Jenkins said with a sly grin. "I had two fly girls I was hittin' on and hardly noticed they had left until it was too late. I ran out into the parking lot, but they were long gone."

"Anyone else leave around then, too?"

"I saw Jacob Boone tearing out of the parking lot when I got outside. And I never found out why either. It was strange."

"Strange how?"

"Strange in that everyone eventually came back and didn't want to talk about what just happened even though we all asked them about it. I guess I know why now."

"Do you remember when everybody left?"

"That was a long time ago, but I want to say it wasn't long after 9:00 p.m. I can't remember exactly when."

Cal shot Kelly a look.

"Thanks, Harold," Cal said. "You've been most helpful."

CHAPTER 34

AFTER LUNCH, CAL AND KELLY DROVE out to Sorghum Lake on the outskirts of the Pickett city limits. It was the local's playground, full of modified boats and pontoon parties. Zipping around the center of the water were the showoffs along with a few people who'd imbibed too much. Cal had no problem distinguishing between the two groups of exhibitionists.

Cal stopped and asked a group of sunbathers if they knew where he might be able to find Jacob Boone. One of the young women laughed and pointed toward the center of the lake.

"If you want to talk with him, better hurry up before he breaks his neck out there," she said.

Cal peered across the lake at a man skiing barefoot. He lasted about six seconds before tumbling across the water and then dipping beneath the surface. When his head re-emerged, he let out a loud yell and threw his fist in the air.

"Is that Jacob Boone out in the center of the lake?" Cal asked, pointing at the man.

"The one and only," she said.

Cal and Kelly walked along the shoreline in an attempt to see where the boat that had since collected Boone out of the water was headed.

"It looks like it's going to that dock over there," Kelly said.

They hustled along the shore in order to meet the boat before it launched out into the lake again for more shenanigans.

As the boat neared the dock, Cal recognized Boone, who had taken over captaining while guzzling a cheap beer. Boone crushed the can with his hand and gave it to a bikini-clad woman. Her big smile indicated that she felt special just to be on board the boat with such a man.

"Think we're going to get anything worthwhile out of Boone now?" Kelly asked.

Cal shrugged. "I guess we're about to find out."

He ambled along the dock with Kelly, stopping a few meters short of where Boone had his fellow boaters tie the vessel off.

"Mr. and Mrs. Murphy," Boone said once he recognized the pair of visitors standing on the dock. "To what do I owe the pleasure of your visit on this beautiful Sunday afternoon?"

"It's a courtesy call," Cal said.

"A courtesy call? What the heck are you talkin' about? You know I don't speak like you city folks."

"I'm working on a story that I plan on running in the next few days, and I want to see if you care to comment on it before *The Seattle Times* publishes it."

"What kind of story?" Boone asked.

Kelly flipped open her iPad and turned it around so Boone could see it.

"The kind of story that accompanies a photo like this," she said.

Boone's eyes widened. "And what kind of caption are

you going to put with that? Hopefully not the kind that will get you sued, right?"

Cal pointed at the image. "If you won't tell us what it's all about, perhaps we'll suggest some possibilities to readers. We've already got several sources on record telling us about a special arrangement you and Sheriff Sloan have. We'd just be reporting what these people said. We'd let the readers make up their own minds."

"That'd be a big mistake then," Boone said.

"Tell us what this is about then," Cal said. "Set the record straight."

"I did some body work for Sheriff Sloan on one of his cars. He always pays me at the race once I've finished getting his car in tip-top shape. It just so happened that he asked me to drive it this year too."

"How convenient," Kelly said.

"Look, if you don't believe me, let's go to my office. I'll show you the receipt right now. But if you don't want to see it, that's your prerogative. But I'll sue you into oblivion if you suggest that I'm doing anything illegal with the sheriff."

"You mean like running moonshine for him?" Cal asked.

Boone chuckled. "Who told you that?"

Cal eyed Boone closely. "Is it true?"

"Is what true?"

"Are you running moonshine with the sheriff's blessing?"

Boone shook his head. "This isn't 1930 or 1950, even. There are far more sophisticated ways to *run moonshine* in the 21st Century ... or so I've heard."

"And this isn't an activity you've been involved with, is it?" Cal said.

"Do you honestly think I'd tell you if I were involved?"

"That's not a denial."

"It's not an admission either," Boone said, throwing his hands in the air. "So, I like to drink and have fun at the lake. I'm a little wild sometimes. But I'm not involved in any illegal activity. That stopped a long time ago. A very long time ago."

Cal continued to press Boone. "Did this illegal activity stop around the time of Susannah Sloan's murder?"

Boone sighed. "Are you kiddin' me?"

"Where were you when Susannah Sloan was killed?"

"I was at the Pirate's Den, drinking with some of my former teammates off the Pickett County High football team. That's it."

"All night?"

"All night."

Kelly leaned forward, hugging her iPad. "That's not what we heard."

Boone let out an exasperated breath. "Fine. You want to hear the truth? I'll tell you the truth. Kill that story you're about to write and meet me for dinner tonight at Curly's around seven. I'll tell you everything then."

Cal and Kelly watched as Boone snatched a beer out of the cooler at the end of the dock before he jumped back into his boat.

"Let's go, boys," Boone said as he fired up the engine. "We've still got plenty of time to make some waves this afternoon."

Boone whipped the boat around toward the center of the lake and pushed the throttle forward, sending the nose of the vessel into the air. A couple of the men on board let out wild yelps. Boone looked over his shoulder at Cal and Kelly, glaring at them.

"Glad we didn't have any dinner plans," Kelly said. "This ought to be interesting."

CHAPTER 35

CAL AND KELLY DECIDED to stop by the Pickett County jail to see if they could chat with Drake. It was a long shot since visiting hours wouldn't begin until Monday afternoon, but Cal was convinced they could talk their way into getting a few minutes with the city's most famous native.

Sheriff Sloan was nowhere to be found, but one of his deputies, Mark Polson, stood watch on the late Sunday afternoon shift.

"Are you sure you can't let us see him?" Kelly asked Deputy Polson.

Polson, who sat at a desk piled high with stacks of files, didn't look up.

"No means no," he muttered.

"Drake's lawyer, Robert Sullivan, is on his way over here," Cal said. "Wouldn't you rather me run interference for you with that pompous jerk?"

Polson sighed and shook his head. "Fine. Just make sure you get me an autograph, will you?" he said, sliding Drake's rookie card across the desk to Cal. "Sheriff Sloan would have my hide if he found out I asked Isaiah Drake for an autograph on anything but an official department form."

"I'll take care of that for you, Deputy," Cal said, picking up the card from the desk.

"Thanks," Polson said. "Follow me." He led Cal and Kelly down a short corridor and then opened a door to an interrogation room. "Wait here while I go get him."

A few minutes later, Polson reappeared with Drake in handcuffs.

"You've got fifteen minutes," Polson said before closing the door and exiting the room.

Drake slumped in a chair across the table from Cal and Kelly.

"What were you thinking?" Cal asked after some awkward silence.

Drake, who'd refused to look up, shook his head.

"I don't know, man. I just knew that Sheriff Sloan was getting away with killing his daughter."

"Do you still think that?" Kelly asked.

"Maybe. I don't know."

"Sullivan is on his way over and should be here within the hour," Cal said.

"On his way over? Where was he?"

"In Savannah," Cal said.

"Playing golf with Hal Golden," Kelly chimed in.

Drake looked up for the first time. "Hal Golden? The prosecutor for my trial?"

Cal nodded. "That's the one."

"I swear I'm gonna—"

"Just chill out," Cal said. "Don't take any physical action, but feel free to fire him. I think he may have been more of a detriment to your case than a help."

Drake leaned forward in his chair. "How so?"

"Sullivan and Golden were buddies in law school."

Drake cocked his head to one side. "Seriously?"

Cal nodded. "I wish it weren't so, but I can't help but feel like they struck some sort of deal on the side. And you got the brunt of it."

"Man, I don't even wanna know."

"You should," Kelly said, "because it's the reason why you spent the last twelve years of your life on death row. It's despicable, really."

Cal flipped a page in his notebook and set his pen down.

"Okay, I need some real talk, right now," he said.

"Shoot."

"Who else can you think of who had a grudge against you and would wish harm on you … or want to frame you for murder?" Cal asked.

Drake sat still for a moment. It was as if he was unsure of what to say—or if he even had an answer. "I didn't really have any enemies other than that lawyer from Jacksonville who was apparently trying to marry my fiancée right out from underneath my nose. But we never met."

"What about Devontae Ray?" Kelly asked.

"The guy in the wheelchair?"

Cal nodded. "That's the one."

"You think he killed Susannah and tried to pin it on me? That's hilarious, really."

"I'm not ruling anything out at the moment," Cal said. "I don't care how absurd it might sound. We have to turn over every rock to get your name cleared."

"Too late for that now after what I did to Sheriff Sloan."

Cal sighed. "Don't be too hard on yourself. I think most judges would have sympathy for you, especially if I testify on your behalf that you were sympathetic when I met with you."

"That'd be mighty nice," Drake said.

"I wouldn't be doing it because it was mighty nice," Cal said. "I'd be doing it because it was the truth, and I'd be remiss if I didn't do the right thing."

"I appreciate it, man."

Kelly shifted in her seat. "Anyone else you can think of? Jacob Boone? Jordan Hayward? Tripp Sloan?"

Drake shook his head. "Why did you even bring up Devontae Ray?"

"Would he have something against you?" Cal asked.

"Maybe."

"Such as . . . ?"

"Such as he hated Susannah for hitting him while he and his brother were riding on a motorcycle. Ray's brother was driving, and he died on the scene. He wasn't wearing a helmet, but I doubt it would've mattered. It was all an accident though."

"Maybe that's not how he saw it," Kelly said.

"No, it was an accident. Susannah could've never done anything to stop it. Never."

"But why try to pin the murder on you?" Cal asked.

"Because he didn't want to go to prison himself."

Cal shrugged. "That's one explanation, but I think it's a weak one. I think there's more to this story."

Drake rubbed his face with his hands.

"Maybe there is," he said.

Cal scratched out a note on his pad. "Go on."

"Devontae's brother and I got busted for robbery when I was like fifteen. Devontae's brother ended up going to prison for it. But I got away with a suspended sentence from Sheriff Sloan. I worked hard to make sure I never did anything like that again."

"And that'd be enough for him to want to see you get locked up for the rest of your life or maybe even die?" Kelly asked.

Drake nodded. "It's quite possible. It ended Devontae's brother's chances at attending Florida State on a football scholarship. It was the summer before classes started in the fall. I was going to be a rising sophomore that year, but not Devontae's brother. He was going to be a senior, the kind who you listened to when he spoke."

"But something happened?"

"Yeah, Drake's brother went to prison while I escaped any semblance of a harsh sentence."

Cal wrote furiously on his pad. "So, do you think there's any possibility that Devontae Ray had *anything* to do with Susannah's death that night … and your framing?"

Drake shook his head. "No way. The dude can't even stand and walk on his own. He would've had to have hired someone to do this to me. And I don't remember any group of people overwhelming me that night."

Cal shrugged. "Maybe you were unconscious."

"I only remember a single hit to the head but never saw anyone's face."

Cal and Kelly both nodded.

"I think we're about to run out of time," Cal said. "But if you think of anyone else, let me know now or forever hold your peace."

"I'm drawing a blank," Drake said. "I can't imagine anyone would want to do that to me."

Cal sighed. "The world has changed. It's far more complex than it ever was from the good ole days. And right now, you're in its cross hairs."

CHAPTER 36

CAL AND KELLY SLIPPED into a booth at Curly's Diner a few minutes before seven and waited for Jacob Boone. Curly brought them their sweet teas and told them he'd put in their usual orders. They both smiled and thanked him.

"Think he's gonna show?" Kelly asked.

Cal sighed. "I hope so. We need answers and soon. If he doesn't, I think he knows he's going to be cast in a very bad light—and he'll only have himself to blame for it."

"Well, I can't wait to get outta here and get back home," Kelly said. "I miss Maddie."

"You're not the only one. Just one look at her face makes me forget about all the vile things in this world," Cal said.

"Yeah, and I think it's high time we start talking about a sister for her."

Cal stared at Kelly. "A sister? Are you sure?"

Kelly nodded enthusiastically. "Come on, Cal. It'll be fun."

"We have vastly different definitions of fun. Functioning on a few hours of sleep each night between feedings and diaper changes is not my idea of fun."

Kelly placed her hand on Cal's. "But that stage doesn't last forever. Besides, don't you want another cute little bundle to hold and cuddle with?"

Cal shot her a look. He knew he was trapped. They'd

232 | R.J. PATTERSON

discussed expanding their family in the past, but this time he felt like he was cornered with only one *right* answer. "I'll think about it."

"What's there to think about? You either want another little precious child or you don't."

"It's not that easy, Kelly. You know that."

"Maddie needs a sister. Maddie *wants* a sister."

"Give me a few days. I can't make a decision like this based solely on emotion, as enticing as it may sound."

Kelly grinned. "I knew you'd come around."

Cal scowled. "I'm thinking about it, not agreeing to anything."

"You will," she said.

Cal looked across the room and noticed Jacob Boone entering the diner.

"Look who's here," Cal said before muttering beneath his breath. "And not a minute too soon."

Kelly playfully hit Cal on the arm. "I heard that."

Cal motioned for Boone to join them, pointing toward the empty seat across from them in the booth.

Boone slid into his seat and interlocked his fingers on the table. "Before we begin, I want to apologize for how I acted earlier," Boone said. "I wasn't exactly myself."

"No apologies necessary," Cal said.

"Okay, fine. Let's get to why we're here."

"Yes, let's do that," Kelly chimed in.

Cal turned his digital recorder on and placed it in the center of the table. "This is all on the record, I trust."

Boone nodded. "The truth is the truth. I'm not afraid of it."

"So, let's hear it. What happened on the night Susannah Sloan was murdered?"

"I wish I had more answers for you," Boone began, "but I'll tell you what I know and everything I saw. On that night, a bunch of us met down at The Pirate's Den for some drinks. I thought it was just going to be a handful of us reliving the good ole days. But it turned into so much more."

"How so?" Cal asked.

"We were all having fun, just talking about our big upset over Ware County, which won the Class 4-A title that year, when all of a sudden the discussion abruptly ended."

"What happened?" Kelly asked.

"Isaiah Drake got up from the table and stormed toward the front door."

"Did you see anything that happened?" Cal asked.

"I saw some guy bump into Drake. He reached in his pocket and pulled out a slip of paper. He looked at it for a few seconds before storming out of the bar."

"Where did he go?"

Boone shrugged. "I wasn't sure at first. But I got up and started to follow him out into the parking lot. When I got outside, I saw him getting into his car. Jordan Hayward ran after him. He got into his car and followed Drake."

"So, what did you do?"

"I climbed into my truck—not my smartest decision of the evening—and went after both of them. I figured they might be going to Susannah Sloan's house, so that's where I drove."

"Why did you think that?" Kelly inquired.

"I think I already mentioned this, but things seemed to be coming to a head with her. She had a full-fledged boyfriend lawyer in Jacksonville along with a couple of side guys."

"Side guys?" Cal asked.

"You know, guys who she was hookin' up with on the side."

"And one of them was Jordan Hayward?" Cal asked.

Boone nodded. "That much was common knowledge, even as everyone in town hoped it wasn't true. Everybody loved Susannah. She was the town sweetheart. But something happened at some point … either that, or there are a bunch of liars in town. Probably a little bit of both as it pertains to what was going on in Pickett."

"What happened next?" Cal asked.

"I drove to Susannah's house and parked a half a block away. I didn't want to raise any suspicion that I was also one of her guys, not that anyone would think that after the way she destroyed my family in court, but more on that in a minute."

"So you go inside and … ?"

"Yeah, I went inside and found Hayward and Drake in Susannah's living room. I grabbed Hayward and told him it was time to leave."

"Did Hayward leave?"

"Not at first, but I coaxed him into coming with me. It was clear from reading Drake's body language that he wanted to be left alone and that Hayward was cramping his style."

"Was Drake trying to be romantic?"

Boone shook his head. "Not from the looks of it. In fact, it seemed like the opposite. He looked angry, but he definitely had something he wanted to say to her that he didn't want anyone else hearing."

"So you just left?"

"It wasn't quite that easy. I had to grab Hayward from behind by his neck at first and then almost bear hug him to get him to leave. He insisted on staying, but I knew that wasn't the smartest move."

"And he eventually went with you?" Kelly asked.

"Yeah," Boone said. "I led Hayward to my truck, and we returned to The Pirate's Den, where we continued to drink."

"Did other people see you?" Cal asked.

"Oh, yeah. It's not like we were hiding in the shadows. Plus, it's difficult to hide when you've got Jordan Hayward with you."

"So, what'd you do after that?"

"After that, we went home to try and sleep off our night of drinking," Boone said. "When we woke up the next morning, it was like a nightmare. One of our own had done the unthinkable—at least, that's what we thought at the time."

"So you're not buying that Drake did it?" Kelly asked.

Boone shook his head. "He loved that girl too much."

"Who do you think could've done it? Sheriff Sloan?"

Boone shrugged. "The Sheriff has been nothin' but good to me since I tried to turn my life around. I don't do drugs anymore and livin' straight and narrow now. I wanted to blame Susannah for all my problems, but she was just doin' her job. I think I could've turned my life around and gotten to a better place with them, but I can't be sure. What I do know is that they all ended up in a good home and are well taken care of. That's all I can ask. It was my fault for doin' such stupid things to begin with. I had to stop blamin' her because I could only blame myself."

"And Sloan helped you through that?" Cal asked.

"Not at first. For the first few weeks after Susannah died, I was glad. I thought it served her right, but then I started to feel bad for some things I said about her to my buddies. I knew it wasn't right the moment it came out of my mouth. That's when I asked Sheriff Sloan if we could talk."

"And he was open to that?"

"He welcomed it and then hired me to work out at his camp, which is why all those nasty rumors got started about me runnin' moonshine for him. They're just ridiculous."

"Hold up," Kelly said. "Sheriff Sloan has a camp? What kind of camp?"

"Camp Manmaker. It's kind of a challenge camp to help older boys who've been struggling in the juvey system. They do tasks together and kind of grow up in the course of a week."

Cal scribbled down some notes. "How long has this camp been going on? And when is it held?"

"It's been goin' on for as long as I can remember," Boone said. "Every summer, he holds several week-long camps. It stays pretty much dormant the rest of the year. We used to hear all kinds of rumors about what really went on there when we were kids, but it's all just a bunch of myths."

"Like the Marsh Monster?" Cal said with a grin.

Boone's face turned serious. "Don't joke about the Marsh Monster. I swear he's real."

"You ever seen him?"

Boone nodded. "Once, when I was on my way back from doin' some work for Sheriff Sloan out at his camp, I saw the Marsh Monster dart across the road in front of my car."

"What'd he look like?"

"It was gettin' dark and I had a hard time makin' out all the details, but he's real. I saw 'em with my own two eyes."

"Okay, okay," Cal said, glancing at his notes. "Let's get back to this Camp Manmaker. So, everything seems on the up and up out there?"

"Sheriff Sloan helped me refocus my life at a time when I needed it most. And for that, I'm eternally grateful. If it weren't for him, I would've probably been dead long ago."

"So if you were building a list of suspects that didn't include Isaiah Drake, who else would you think could have killed Susannah Sloan?"

"What about the dude she was gonna marry? You know, that lawyer schmuck from Jacksonville?" Boone offered.

"He had an airtight alibi," Kelly said. "He was at a fundraiser that night and was there long after midnight. No way he could've done it."

Boone slapped the table with open palms. "Well, you've got me then. I've got no idea who could've done it. Sheriff Sloan is the only one who could cover up a crime in this town—and I just can't believe he did it."

Cal offered his hand to Boone, who shook it.

"Thanks for all your help and your openness," Cal said.

"My pleasure. I hope you catch the bastard who did this to Susannah. For a while, I thought she did me wrong, but I know better now. She didn't deserve to end up like this."

"Ma'am," Boone said as he tipped his cap to Kelly.

Cal waited until Boone exited the diner before saying a word.

"Well?" Call said.

"Well, what?" Kelly asked.

"Well, what do you think? Did we finally get someone in this town to tell us the truth about what happened that night?"

"Even if we did, how can we verify it? Of the other four people who were there, two are now dead, one is the sheriff, and the other man claims to not remember a thing."

"Maybe we can jog his memory."

Cal's phone buzzed. He held up the screen so Kelly could see it.

"Look, it's Jarrett Anderson," Cal said before answering the call. "Agent Anderson, what in the world are you doing calling me on a Sunday evening?"

"Are you still in Pickett?" Anderson asked.

"How'd you—?"

"I read your story today," Anderson said. "I still keep up with you from time to time."

"Well, I'm honored that you care that much."

"You write sports here in Seattle. You don't think I'm going to read the political section, do you?"

"Good point."

"Anyway, I was calling to let you know that I heard there's a big raid going down around Pickett tonight."

"What kind of raid? Does it have to do with my story?"

"I'm not sure. One of my friends from way back in Quantico told me that they're onto some crime ring."

"It wouldn't happen to involve a guy going by the name of the Enforcer, would it?" Cal asked.

"Actually, I think that's the name he mentioned—just thought you'd want a heads up, okay?"

"Got any idea where this is going down?"

"I didn't get any details like that, but I know it's somewhere near where you're at."

"Thanks, Agent Anderson. I appreciate it."

Cal hung up and looked at Kelly. "We're sitting on a powder keg here, and it's about to blow."

"That bad, huh?" she asked.

Cal nodded slowly.

"So, am I just gonna sit here and watch you finish your fries or are we going to go watch the fireworks?"

"Grab your coat. We're going to Camp Manmaker."

Cal stood up and turned around, only to be met by Crazy Corey Taylor.

"I wouldn't do that if I were you," Taylor said, shaking his index finger in Cal's face.

Cal drew back. "Excuse me, but I need to get going."

"Not if you think going to Camp Manmaker is a good idea."

Cal turned sideways to shimmy past Taylor.

"I don't really have time for this," Cal said as he grabbed Kelly's hand and headed for the door.

"Don't say I didn't warn you," Taylor called out after them.

It was the last thing Cal heard before the glass door to Curly's Diner banged shut and silenced Taylor's words on the sidewalk outside.

Cal looked over his shoulder and back into the restaurant.

"Don't go there," Taylor mouthed as he waved his hands. "Don't do it."

"Think we should listen to him?" Kelly asked. "He seems kind of adamant about us not going."

"We've got to get back to Seattle before Buckman cancels the company credit card on us for running up the expense account. Plus, I've got to write this monstrous story sooner rather than later. All this research isn't going to amount to much if this story takes off."

"I hope you're right, Cal," she said. "But I've got a feeling we should trust Crazy Corey Taylor for once."

CHAPTER 37

CAL LOOKED UP CAMP MANMAKER on his phone and found a map to the location. In a matter of minutes, he and Kelly had exited the city limits of Pickett and were hurtling down a two-lane blacktop that skirted the Okefenokee. The sun had started to dip on the horizon, and Cal estimated they had a half hour of daylight remaining.

Five minutes later, they reached the turnoff point for the camp, the sign nearly covered up by a cluster of kudzu. Cal wheeled his car onto the dirt driveway as per the directions on his phone and continued along. Spanish moss hung from the bald-cypress nestled into the swampy areas on both sides of the road. Black gum trees dominated the drier landscape, and the frogs provided an unrelenting chorus. Cal rolled his window down to take in the swamp air, which smelled musky and pungent.

"Put that window up," Kelly said, playfully gagging.

"What? You don't like the fresh smell of a pole cat?" Cal asked.

"I told you we should've listened to Crazy Corey Taylor."

Cal smiled as the car bumped along the road. He was enjoying the comedic moment in what had been an otherwise serious and grueling week of interviews and research in a town that held his intentions suspect. He wasn't sure what he was going to find at Camp Manmaker, but he wanted to see it for himself and get Kelly to snap a few photos in the evening light for the story. If anything, an aside about the camp promised to provide interesting insight into the man behind the badge.

Cal finally reached a row of cabins and what looked like a main meeting hall. He parked the car and got out. Kelly lagged a minute behind as she gathered her camera gear.

"I didn't picture a place like this," Cal said. "Did you?"

Kelly lugged her bag toward Cal and shook her head.

"I figured it would've been somewhat run down, but this place is kind of nice."

"Maybe that's how this camp works. They work hard and part of what they do is keep it up."

Cal walked around the grounds, inspecting the buildings a little closer. He cupped his hands around his face and peered into the windows.

"I can't really see much inside," Cal said.

"Did you try the door to see if it's open?" Kelly asked while she snapped several pictures.

Cal jogged over to the door to one of the cabins and jiggled the handle. It was locked.

"Nothing," he said.

Cal joined Kelly as she started to walk deeper into the grounds and then Cal froze.

"Look over there," Cal said in a strained whisper. "Sloan's truck. If he catches us, he's liable to throw us in a cell right next to Drake."

Kelly shot him a look. "I told you we should've listened to Crazy Corey Taylor."

"Fine. You're right. We shouldn't have come."

Daylight had given way to dusk, making it easier to see a light in one of the cabins about three hundred meters away through the trees.

"What do you think is over there?" Kelly asked.

"Seriously? A cabin in the middle of nowhere near a backwoods town? And you want to go there?" Cal asked.

"Aren't you the least bit curious?"

"Of course I am, but I'm not interested in getting into trouble here tonight," Cal said, "especially after we've been able to avoid it for about a week."

Fireflies started to flicker as they ascended toward the top of the slash pines scattered around the grounds. The chorus of the frogs bellowing seemed to grow louder.

"Since when did you lose your nerve to go the extra mile on a story like this?" Kelly asked.

Cal sighed. "Did I ever tell you that you're a bad influence on me?"

He spun toward the cabin with Kelly walking by his side. Her wide grin took the place of any words she could've offered up at the time. And Cal reveled in it, reminding himself how lucky he was to have a woman as committed to good journalism as he was—maybe even more so. She was also just as curious as he was, story or not.

Cal and Kelly stayed low to the ground as they approached the sole lit cabin. As they got closer, Cal realized it wasn't like the other cabins. It was set farther back and appeared to be built more recently. Instead of a tin roof, it had a shingled one. And the façade wasn't wood but brick.

Once they reached the structure, Cal put his finger to his lips and then motioned for Kelly to follow him to the back. With a set of steps on both sides of the building that led up to the door, the windows sat high off the ground but not so high that Cal and Kelly couldn't see inside.

When Cal got close enough and peered into the window, his eyes widened. He then slunk down against the side of the building.

"What is it?" Kelly whispered.

"See for yourself."

Cal watched as she followed his instructions only to join him seconds later.

"What's going on in there?" she asked.

"Sshh," Cal said, putting his finger to his lips.

"It looks like they're about to go to war in there."

"And distribute several kilos of drugs to everyone in Pickett County."

Cal stood up again to make sure he wasn't imagining things. But nothing had changed. All types of guns were spread out over one table. In the center of the room were duffle bags with stacks of cash. And against the far wall was a table piled high with drugs sealed in tight clear packets. The contents were almost so astonishing that Cal hardly took time to note all of the people inside. He only remembered seeing Sheriff Sloan along with about a half dozen others.

Cal decided to stand up once more to see if he recognized anyone else.

This time, the room was empty.

Cal heard a click behind him and froze.

"I told you and told you and told you to leave town," boomed Sloan. "But did you listen to me? Nooo. You had to try to be some hero in your own stupid story. But now you're just going to end up dead. And all because you didn't listen to me."

Cal raised his hands and turned around slowly.

"Look, why don't you just let us leave now, and we'll forget we ever saw anything?" Cal said.

"I've got a better idea," Sloan said. "First, I'll take your camera and destroy it. Then I'll drop you off in Alligator Alley with your hands and feet tied together. How's that sound?"

"Sounds like murder," Kelly grumbled.

Sloan chuckled. "Sounds like a better idea than yours. Now stand up and start walkin'."

Cal kept his hands in the air as he stumbled along the path toward Sloan's truck. While Cal's predicament looked bleak, the only thing he could do to buy them more time was to talk with Sloan. Plus, if Cal was going to die, he at least wanted to know why Sloan killed his daughter—or why he helped cover it up.

"I can appreciate you wanting to murder us, I—"

Sloan clucked his tongue. "Let's not use the *M* word around here, okay? Nobody is going to get murdered around here, you understand? You might get eaten by somethin', but not murdered."

"One of your Marsh Monsters going to get us?" Kelly asked.

Sloan broke into a guffaw.

"You Yankees always eat that story up," he said.

"Based on my interviews, sounds like the rest of your town has too," Cal snapped.

"Oh, they all know it's good for business, good for the tourism dollars down this way. Just about every enterprisin' resident of Pickett County has created some kind of Marsh Monster memorabilia, and they peddle it whenever there's a sightin'." He paused. "And there just might be a sightin' tonight."

Cal stumbled forward in the dark, the tip of Sloan's gun pressed against Cal's back as a constant reminder that the end was undoubtedly near. He thought about Kelly, who held his hand tightly, and little Maddie, who would grow up without a father. All the emotions accompanying such thoughts rose up within him—along with the desire to not give up. He had to try something, anything to stall or maneuver himself into a position to make a getaway or at least help Kelly do so.

But in the moment, all he could think to do was keep asking questions.

"So why'd you do it?" Cal asked.

"Do what?" Sloan said.

"Kill your own daughter?"

Sloan exhaled. "That's where you're all wrong there, Mr. Murphy. I never killed my daughter. And I think we both know who's responsible for that—the crazy lunatic that attacked me at my house yesterday. I hope they put him on a fast track to execution after he gets convicted a second time."

Cal kept walking, squeezing Kelly's hand. "I know you went to see her that night. We spoke with a witness who saw you there."

"I didn't kill her," Sloan growled.

"So, what did you have to hide?" Kelly asked, apparently emboldened by Cal's line of questioning.

"That was a long time ago, but you're right, I did go see her about a private matter for a few minutes and then I left."

"Where'd you go after that?"

"You reporters are always stickin' your nose where it don't belong. But what does it matter? You're about to become a casualty of the dangerous wildlife livin' in the Okefenokee in a few hours anyway. I guess it can't hurt to satisfy that curiosity itch of yours. Maybe you can think about it as you lie on the ground, bleeding out from a vicious gator attack."

Cal shook his head. "You gonna tell me or just drone on about how torturous you're going to make our deaths?"

"I was havin' an affair with Mrs. Elaine Butterfield, the wife of Pickett's mayor at the time. And I didn't want him to find out."

"Is that the personal matter you went to talk to your daughter about? Your affair?"

"That's somethin' that will stay between the two of us," Sloan said before shoving Cal to the ground. "Tie him up, boys."

Three of the men with Sloan rushed to the ground and bound Cal's hands together before also binding his feet.

"Now the woman," Sloan commanded.

In less than a minute, Kelly was also tied up like Cal.

"What are you gonna do with us?" Cal asked.

Even in the twilight, Cal could see Sloan's teeth glistening as he grinned.

"I'm gonna introduce you to the Marsh Monster."

CHAPTER 38

CAL MOANED AS SLOAN'S THUGS flung him into the back of a pickup truck. They had the decency to handle Kelly with a little more care, but not much more. His face rested on the bed of the truck as he looked over at her. In the pale moonlight, he could see a tear streaking down her face.

"It's gonna be all right," he said. "Trust me."

She closed her eyes tight and exhaled, remaining silent. Cal was certain it was because she didn't believe him. And he couldn't really blame her either. The situation appeared dire. Death was almost certainly imminent.

The truck roared to life and began to bump along the dirt road toward the main highway. Cal contemplated jumping out for a second but knew he couldn't get far. It'd only hasten his demise. He could only pray—and hope.

After a few minutes, the truck slowed down. Cal would've sworn that it was because they'd reached the main road. But then he saw the flashing lights.

Cal struggled to sit up as he heard the hum of several engines toward the front of the truck. Then a voice over a bull horn.

"Step out of the vehicle with your hands up," boomed a voice.

Cal listened as the doors to the truck flew open and shots were exchanged. He counted two men crying out in pain before bodies hit the ground. Then he heard an all-too familiar voice in Sheriff Sloan.

"No need to shoot," Sloan said. "I surrender."

Cal struggled to get to his knees so he could peer around the outside of the truck bed to see what was going on. Once he did, he realized that it was over for Sloan.

"Sheriff Sloan, you're under arrest," one of the agents said.

"What for?"

"Possession of narcotics with intent to distribute, money laundering, and tax evasion, among other things."

Sloan sneered.

"This'll never stand up in court, and you know it," he said.

One of the agents began to read Sloan his Miranda Rights.

"Check the far cabin," Cal yelled. "And add kidnapping to the list."

A pair of agents rushed over and untied Cal and Kelly and began interviewing them. Meanwhile, an FBI vehicle kicked up a cloud of dust as it headed toward the Camp Manmaker facilities.

"You better hope I don't get convicted," Sloan said as he looked at Cal. "I will find you."

An agent jerked Sloan toward one of the black SUVs blocking the way of Sloan's truck. "Let's go, *Enforcer*."

"Good thing I turned on the recorder on my phone," Cal said. "Have a nice life."

An FBI agent interviewed Cal and Kelly while they waited for the other team of agents to return from inspecting the cabin. When the agents finally returned, more agents piled into the vehicle and headed back toward the cabin.

"Sheriff Sloan is the *Enforcer*?" Cal asked, still shocked at the suggestion.

The agent nodded. "Don't worry. Sloan and the rest of these guys will never see the light of day again … unless it's the inside of a prison yard. But there's one more guy in this ring we've yet to identify who doesn't appear to be here tonight."

"What's his name?"

"His handle in the group is *Monster*. Ever heard of him?"

"Nope," Cal said.

He then turned and looked at Kelly, whose tear-stained cheeks had almost dried.

"I told you it would be all right," Cal said.

"You got lucky," she said.

"Maybe, but I was still right."

She forced a smile. "But there's just one thing."

"What's that?"

"We still don't know who killed Susannah Sloan?"

Cal broke into a faint smile. "That's my girl."

CHAPTER 39

ON MONDAY, CAL AND KELLY checked out of the Okefenokee Inn. They had a direct flight out of Atlanta to Seattle on Tuesday morning, but Cal wanted to get an early jump and clean up a few loose ends before they returned home. He figured they'd overstayed their welcome in Pickett by a few days at least, long enough to see the long-time sheriff arrested by federal agents and a big drug ring busted. But it still didn't answer the question Cal and Kelly had traveled to Pickett to get for the long feature on Isaiah Drake: Who killed Susannah Sloan?

Cal and Kelly agreed that their first order of business would be to stop by the Pickett County Sheriff's Department and see if they could speak with Drake one final time. When they arrived, Drake was in the lobby, signing some paperwork with his lawyer, Robert Sullivan.

"Like that, I'm free?" Drake asked, somewhat bewildered.

Deputy Blake Tillman, who was serving as the acting sheriff, nodded.

"Apparently, there were no witnesses who were willing to testify against you, so I saw to it that you were released without any charges," Tillman said. "I apologize for the inconvenience and any discomfort this may have caused you."

Drake turned around to recognize Cal and Kelly. Gone was Drake's anger they'd witnessed at Sheriff Sloan's house or the bitterness that consumed him in prison a week ago. And Drake's drastically different demeanor startled Cal.

"You look … at peace," Cal said.

Drake nodded. "I am, thanks to you and Kelly and The Innocence Alliance. I feel like I have a legitimate shot to clear my name. I'll never get my NFL career back, but my name is more important anyway, right?"

Cal and Kelly both nodded.

"I'm glad we could help," Kelly said.

"What will you do now?" Cal asked.

"I'm going to develop a plan for moving forward and come up with a strategy for winning the next trial."

"If there is one," Tillman chimed in.

Drake spun around. "What do you mean?"

"You're only going to be re-tried if another suspect isn't found," Tillman said.

"And is there one?" Cal asked.

Tillman shook his head. "Not that I'm aware of, but you never know. Stranger things have happened, so good luck."

"I'm not going to count on luck," Drake said. "It played a role in getting me out of prison, but only after twelve years. I'm not too excited about the prospect of relying on it to help me avoid returning there."

Cal asked Drake a few questions before shaking hands and waving goodbye. Drake grabbed Cal and hugged him, catching him off guard. When he looked into Drake's watery eyes, Cal realized it was a sincere emotion.

"You helped me get my life back," Drake said. "Thank you."

Cal smiled. "It was my pleasure, though I'm not sure I

did that much. Just try not to wave any more guns in the faces of any other sheriffs." He winked at Tillman, who nodded back knowingly.

"I promise I won't," Drake said.

"And if you ever need anything, please call me at the paper," Cal said. "I'll be honored to help you in any way that I can."

Drake shook Cal's and Kelly's hands before exiting the office.

Cal turned and looked at Tillman.

"Why'd you do that?" Cal asked.

"He'd already been through enough, not to mention that we just might learn that Sheriff Sloan was the one who deserved to be in jail all those years, not Isaiah Drake," Tillman said.

"You're gonna make a great sheriff," Cal said.

"Thanks. And if you ever need anything, please call me," Tillman said as he handed his business card to Cal. It already had the word Sheriff printed beneath his name instead of Deputy.

"Wow," Cal said as he studied the card. "You work fast."

Tillman grinned. "I dream big, my friend."

Cal and Kelly exited the building only to be accosted by Crazy Corey Taylor within seconds.

"So, did ya figure out who killed Susannah Sloan yet?" Taylor asked.

Cal and Kelly both shook their heads.

"Are you ready to find out?" he asked, flashing his toothy grin.

Cal sighed and looked down at the ground before glancing up at Taylor.

"Lay it on me," Cal said. "What do I have to lose?"

"I have a picture I want to show you," Taylor said as he clutched a small photo tight against his chest. "I showed it to Sheriff Sloan during the investigation, but he didn't wanna listen to me. But I think you will … and I think you'll take me seriously, too."

"Let's see it," Cal said.

Taylor slowly pulled the picture away from his chest and held it out for Cal and Kelly to see.

"Is that who I think it is?" Cal asked.

Taylor nodded. "Sure is."

"That can't be him," Kelly said, almost unable to utter the words.

"Don't question me," Taylor said. "I'm just the messenger who took this picture."

"When did you take it?" Cal asked.

"About twelve years ago. Not a soul in town believed me when I told them. Guess that's what happens when they all think you're on the crazy train."

Cal looked at Kelly. "I guess we have one more stop before we leave town. Wait right here."

Hustling back into the Pickett County Sheriff's Department, Cal flagged down Tillman.

"About getting your help if we ever needed anything," Cal said. "I think we need your help now."

CHAPTER 40

CAL AND KELLY KNOCKED and waited outside the door of Devontae Ray's house. A stiff breeze whipped a few stray pieces of trash into the air, carrying them twenty or thirty meters a clip before briefly touching down and then repeating the dance all over again. A robin chirped peacefully in a nearby tree. Cal noted the ramp leading up over the house steps and onto the porch needed a fresh coat of paint as it had started to chip along the edges.

Cal listened to see if Ray was home. After about a minute, he heard the heavy roll of a wheelchair making its way through the house. The rolling noise finally came to a stop and was followed by a soft bump against the door. A slit in the middle of the door opened up.

"What do *you* want?" Ray asked.

"Hi, Mr. Ray. My wife and I are about to head back to Seattle in about an hour, but we wanted to ask you a few questions first," Cal said as he bent down to see Ray's face through the slot in the door.

"Why don't I save you two an hour and let you get on your way?" Ray said. The slit closed.

"I think I figured out that Jordan Hayward killed Susannah Sloan, and we wanted to ask you about it."

The slot re-opened.

"Why do you think I'd know anything about it?" Ray asked.

"I don't, but I know you knew Jordan Hayward."

A few locks slid and turned before the door swung open. Ray sat hunched over in his wheelchair. He gestured for them to come inside.

"I appreciate this," Cal said as he and Kelly entered the house. "Is there a place where we can sit down and talk?"

Ray glared at him. "I'm always sittin' down, and I rarely have visitors, so I don't really think about it much." He sighed. "Let's go to the kitchen. It's not comfortable seating—from what I hear—but it'll suffice."

Kelly fidgeted with a small packet in her hand.

"Do you mind if I boil some water?" she asked. "I've got a medicine I need to take with this special tea."

Ray scowled. "What kind of medicine is *that*?"

"It's a homeopathic medicine?"

"A homeo-*what*? Oh, forget it. Sure. There are pots down below, of course."

Kelly dug out a pot, filled it with water, and put it on the stove. She cranked the burner up to high and took a seat at the table.

"I'm not sure I can really provide much for you," Ray said. "But I guess I can try. I just don't have long."

"Oh, this won't take long," Cal said. "Just a few questions about the night of May 7, 2004. Do you remember where you were?"

"Is that the night Susannah Sloan was killed?" Ray asked. Cal nodded.

"In that case, I was doin' nothin', just like every other night in my life since my accident."

Cal scribbled down a note. "I heard about your accident. What happened?"

"Susannah wasn't payin' attention, and she plowed right into me and my brother on his motorcycle. The docs said I was lucky to be alive, but I'm not so sure I was the lucky one between me and my brother. Do you have any idea what it's like to live like this, strapped into a wheelchair every single day? It's tiresome, I tell you."

"I can only imagine," Cal said.

"How'd you feel about Ms. Sloan after that?" Kelly asked.

Ray sneered. "I hated her guts for a long time, but eventually I got over it. I finally made peace with the fact that I'd never be able to walk or run again. It's not the best hand you can get dealt in life, but it's the only one I got, so I try to make the best of it. Over time, I eventually just forgot about Susannah and went on with my life."

"Until she died?" Cal asked.

"Yeah, when she died, it brought back all those painful memories again—then I was glad she was dead. She only escaped because her daddy was the sheriff. Otherwise, she would've and should've gone to jail. But whatever, it's over and done with."

"I heard you got in trouble with the law before that," Cal said. "What kept you from entering a life of crime?"

Ray flashed a faint smile. "Believe it or not, it was Sheriff Sloan himself. I went to Camp Manmaker one summer, and it helped keep me straight. That and my momma, God rest her soul."

"What happened to your mother?" Kelly asked.

"She died of lung cancer. Couldn't stop smokin', even after they told her she was dyin' from it. I know she's in a better place now."

The pot started to boil. Kelly got up and walked to the stove.

"Where do you keep your mugs?" Kelly asked.

"Down below with everything else," Ray said. "Look in the cabinet next to the refrigerator."

Kelly knelt down and pulled out a coffee mug. She put it on the table and proceeded to fetch the water. She poured the hot water over the tea bag.

"Smells good," Ray said.

"Yeah, but it needs to steep for a few minutes," she said as she finished pouring. "Waiting is the worst part about making such delicious smelling tea."

Then Kelly, still carrying the pot of hot water, lurched toward Ray, sending the hot water flying toward him.

"Look out," Kelly cried.

Ray leaped out of his wheelchair, jumping to the side as he watched the water splash onto the kitchen floor. Then he slowly looked up at Cal and Kelly.

"Well, isn't this interesting," Cal said.

Ray reached behind his back and pulled out a gun, training it on Cal and Kelly. He motioned for Kelly to move closer to Cal.

"It most certainly is," Ray said. "Looks like you're gonna miss your flight."

"If you plan on killing us, please make it quick, but only after you tell me how you did it," Cal said.

Ray furrowed his brow. "Did what?"

"How you murdered Susannah Sloan?"

"I shot her at point blank range, just like I'm gonna do to you."

"Why? Were you still bitter about her running you over and never having to suffer any consequences?" Cal asked, pressing Ray.

"Believe it or not, it was a simple hit."

"A hit? What are you talking about?"

Ray shook his head. "Don't act like you don't know. I heard about your little stunt last night at Camp Manmaker. You know what goes on there."

Cal nodded. "So, what? She found out that her father was a big drug lord in South Georgia?"

"Pretty much. Sheriff Sloan tried to convince her to leave it alone and help throw the feds off his trail. She told him she wouldn't do that, so he told me to convince her by any means necessary. I don't think he meant for me to kill her, but I did. In the end, what was he going to say. He would've gone to jail for life if he tried to turn on me—and he knew it."

"So he told you *that night* to take care of her?"

"Naw, this had been in the works for a few days. He just stopped by her house to plead with her one more time and give her one more chance. When I heard that Isaiah Drake was going to be in town, I decided to pin it all on him. And he'd be dead and this case would've been long gone if it hadn't been for you."

"You were the one who planted that picture in Drake's pocket?"

Ray smiled and stroked his chin.

"That punk did exactly what I wanted him to. Drake made it so easy for me to pin the murder on him. I snuck up behind him, and he never knew what hit him. I gave him something that knocked him out for hours and planted everything on him before I shoved him out in that johnboat, right where that idiot deputy Tate Pellman went fishing every weekend."

Ray cocked his gun and pointed it at Cal's head. "Any more questions before I end this little game?"

"And the finger?" Kelly asked.

"My special little touch."

"Just one more," Cal said. "Why'd you fake it? Why stay in a wheelchair all these years?"

"Because nobody would believe I could be capable of such things, especially being the Marsh Monster or just *The Monster*, depending on who you're talkin' to."

"But what about—?"

"I'm done with your questions," Ray said. "Time to bury you in the swamp."

Before Ray could move, the front door flew open and a team of Pickett County deputies swarmed into the room.

"Drop your gun, nice and easy," Tillman said. "Your little charade is over, Devontae."

Ray placed his gun on the floor and raised his hands in the air.

"Good luck in court," Cal said before adding with a wink, "and thanks for the great story."

CHAPTER 41

ON FRIDAY MORNING, Cal was barely awake when Maddie came bounding into his room. She jumped on top of him and begged him to play. Cal moaned for a moment before he stretched and got up. If it was up to him, he would've rather slept for another two hours, but he realized he couldn't waste any opportunity to spend with his family, especially his sweet daughter.

He glanced next to him and realized Kelly was gone. Making his way into the living room with Maddie in tow, Cal savored the aroma of a freshly brewed cup of tea. Kelly, who was smiling in the kitchen, joined him, carrying a mug for him as well.

"I made you a cup," she said. "It's not sweet tea, of course, but it tastes almost as good."

"Thanks," Cal said, taking the cup from her hand.

After taking a few sips, he set the cup down on the coffee table in the center of the room and proceeded to play with Maddie. He started out with a game of "Ride a Little Pony" before branching off into his favorite derivative of the game, "Ride a Big Elephant," which was a wild adventure through the jungle that ended with her swinging from vine to vine.

"Look, Mom," she shouted. "I'm Tarzan."

Kelly laughed and set a copy of the morning paper on the couch next to Cal before whisking Maddie into the air and spinning her around.

"I thought you might want to read that," Kelly said.

Cal glanced down at the paper. The front page, above the fold, blared the headline *Free at Last* followed by the long subhead *The curious tale of how Isaiah Drake went from beloved to hated to condemned to cleared—and how he plans to get his life back.*

"Everything was stacked against him. I can't believe the truth finally came out," Cal said aloud, though Kelly didn't hear him as she was preoccupied with Maddie.

He smiled as he watched the scene in front of him.

Cal's phone then buzzed. It was Marsha Frost from The Innocence Alliance.

"Ms. Frost," Cal began, "how are you this morning?"

"Honestly, Cal?" she said.

"I only deal in truth."

"I'm crying my eyes out. Your article this morning was moving. What a story. I'm so glad I called you and asked for your help. We hardly had to do any work. You did all the heavy lifting."

Cal chuckled. "Don't make me out to be a hero. I just did my job. It's what any tenacious journalist would've done."

"Key word there is *tenacious*."

"There are more of us there than you think, trust me."

"Well, I wanted to make sure you knew I appreciated it. We can't exactly take much credit for Isaiah Drake's exoneration, but we don't exactly do this for the glory or the acclaim."

"You just do it because it's right."

"Yes—and thank you again."

"Any time."

Cal hung up and scanned the article. He enjoyed seeing his articles in print far more over seeing them on the Internet. There was just something about the printed word on physical paper that made whatever he wrote feel like a bigger deal than appearing on just a website.

He re-read the section about the Georgia Bar opening up an investigation into Hal Golden and Robert Sullivan.

Nobody got away with anything.

At the end of the story, he re-read the part about Drake starting the Susannah Sloan Foundation, a non-profit designed to provide scholarships and support for aspiring prosecutors.

Cal couldn't help but smile: an innocent man was free because of him and a handful of guilty ones were behind bars.

He walked across the room and noticed a white envelope with his name scrawled across the front.

"What's this, hun?" Cal asked.

"Oh, I forgot to tell you about that," Kelly said. "It was stuck in the door when I woke up this morning to go get the paper."

Cal opened the note and quickly broke into a wide grin.

Inside was Drake's signed rookie card, a gift certificate, and a short note. It read:

> Mr. Murphy,
>
> I'll never be able to thank you and your wife enough for the beautiful gift you've given me—the gift of a new start on life. I never thought much about life beyond football since that was taken away from me. And

to be perfectly honest, I never thought much about my future at all since I didn't think I'd have one.

While I have no idea what I'm going to do next, I know that I want to do it with the same passion and fervor that you do your job. Your article captured my struggle so perfectly. I wept as I read it, just like I have many times over the past few days. Take Kelly out to dinner and know that if you ever need my help with anything, I'll be there for you.

Forever your friend,
Isaiah Drake #34

THE END

ACKNOWLEDGMENTS

THERE ARE ALWAYS SO MANY people to thank when embarking on a writing project, but I must start somewhere. And I'll start with Margo Yoder, who helped shape this story into something better through her keen eye for detail, as well as Krystal Wade, whose editing skills helped take this wrinkled shirt of a story and press it smooth. And Dan Pitts did another wonderful job in capturing the look and feel of the south Georgia town which this story was based on for the cover.

Bill Cooper continues to crank out stellar audio versions of all my books — and I have no doubt that this will yield the same high-quality listening enjoyment.

And to you the reader—thanks for reading!

ABOUT THE AUTHOR

R.J. PATTERSON is an award-winning writer living in southeastern Idaho. He first began his illustrious writing career as a sports journalist, recording his exploits on the soccer fields in England as a young boy. Then when his father told him that people would pay him to watch sports if he would write about what he saw, he went all in. He landed his first writing job at age 15 as a sports writer for a daily newspaper in Orangeburg, S.C. He later earned a degree in newspaper journalism from the University of Georgia, where he took a job covering high school sports for the award-winning *Athens Banner-Herald* and *Daily News*.

He later became the sports editor at a daily newspaper in south Georgia before working in the magazine world as an editor and freelance journalist. He has won numerous writing awards, including a national award for his investigative reporting on a sordid tale surrounding an NCAA investigation over the University of Georgia football program.

R.J. enjoys the great outdoors of the Northwest while living there with his wife and three children. He still follows sports closely.

He also loves connecting with readers and would love to hear from you. To stay updated about future projects, connect with him over Facebook or on the Internet at www.RJPbooks.com

Made in the USA
San Bernardino, CA
17 November 2019